W9-BUK-024

## DERRINGER DANGER

Buckskin took a shot. The man turned, fear on his face, and kicked his mount in the sides and plunged harder down the slope. Buckskin's shot missed. He continued the chase. Ahead he heard a scream, then the piercing cry of a wounded horse.

He slowed his mount and edged through another curtain of heavy brush and small aspen. Just in front of him, the ground fell away into a forty-foot-deep canyon.

Where was the rider?

He frowned, then looked at the leafy form of the tree halfway down the embankment. Some of the leaves moved. Then the whole top of the tree quivered and trembled.

Buckskin put a .45 slug into the tree behind the man and shouted, "That's far enough. Move another inch downward and I'll cut you in half with forty-five slugs."

Also in the *Buckskin* Series:

## BUCKSKIN #38
# DERRINGER DANGER

# KIT DALTON

LEISURE BOOKS  NEW YORK CITY

A LEISURE BOOK®

May 2006

Published by

Dorchester Publishing Co., Inc.
200 Madison Avenue
New York, NY 10016

If you purchased this book without a cover you should be aware
that this book is stolen property. It was reported as "unsold and
destroyed" to the publisher and neither the author nor the publisher
has received any payment for this "stripped book."

Copyright © 1993 by Chet Cunningham/BookCrafters

All rights reserved. No part of this book may be reproduced or
transmitted in any form or by any electronic or mechanical means,
including photocopying, recording or by any information storage
and retrieval system, without the written permission of the
publisher, except where permitted by law.

ISBN 0-8439-3587-1

The name "Leisure Books" and the stylized "L" with design are
trademarks of Dorchester Publishing Co., Inc.

Printed in the United States of America.

Visit us on the web at www.dorchesterpub.com.

# DERRINGER
# DANGER

# Chapter One

Buckskin Lee Morgan stared at the man, not quite believing what the rancher had said.

"Wait a minute. You mean there's no job for me here? You caught the two rustlers and hung them a week ago?"

The big rancher from the Circle Z grinned. "Damned if we didn't, Morgan. Hung them two bastards on Main Street in town and left them spinning in the wind for a whole damn week before the Preacher made us cut them down. We sent a damn clear message to cattle rustlers in this part of Wyoming that they're facing the short end of a rope if'n they get caught stealing our beef."

"But I came from Denver to take this job," Buckskin said. "Spent my last dollar getting here. Bought this broken down horse at Rock Springs. She's used up by now, worthless."

"Sorry, no job. Told you in the wire the job was open when you got here if we hadn't caught them. Sorry, now we can't use your detective talents. We just plain don't need no range detective no more."

"I'll have to charge you my expenses. I came in good faith. You hired me in that telegram. You owe me sixty-five dollars."

The rancher chuckled and sent a spurt of tobacco juice at a grasshopper that had landed six feet away on the brown dirt of the ranch yard.

"Mister, you go ahead and charge me all you want. I ain't gonna pay it. You might as well ride back to Rock Springs far as I see."

Buckskin scowled. Things hadn't been going well lately. He'd had that problem in Salt Lake City, and then the job in Denver didn't pan out. He'd been on a long string of bad luck. His once fat bank account had dropped to a big zero; actually he was $35 overdrawn at his Denver bank.

"You need another cow hand? I can earn my pay. I really need a job of some kind about now."

"Sorry. Our spring roundup is over and things are settling down. Might try the Bar L south about twenty miles."

"What's to the north?"

"Not one hell of a lot. Couple of good sized herds up around Jackson, but that's near eighty miles to the north. Two small outfits along the trail, but not much hope there."

The rancher shook his head. "Sorry about this. You come have some dinner with the men at the bunk house 'fore you ride out. Give you the grub line benefit anyhow."

Buckskin ate all he could that noon at the heavily laden table, then rode north. It was sparse, Wyoming country. Some range of the Rocky Mountains reared up to the east of him and another range soared into the sky fifty or sixty miles to the west. The Shining Mountains he'd heard them called. He'd be riding between them moving northwest toward Jackson.

Eighty miles, a good two days. He might be lucky and find a rancher who would feed him. If not, he'd feast on rabbit. He'd seen several on his ride this far.

By sundown that first afternoon on the trail, he'd made only fifteen miles and hadn't seen a rabbit since he left the last ranch. He had a chew on jerky from his saddlebags and some water from a small stream and bedded down off the trail.

The next morning he came to a small ranch. It was a one man operation, but he made a try. The rancher and his wife assured him they needed a hired hand but couldn't afford to pay. They fed him and he moved on.

It was the middle of the third day when he approached Jackson, Wyoming. He'd followed the surging Snake River for several miles. It had created a wide green valley that looked like prime grazing land. He saw dozens of cattle working the grass but he didn't get close enough to check on brands.

Farther north, through the valley and to the west, he could see the snowcapped peaks the early French trappers had called the Grand Tetons. Literally, the French words meant big tits. They surged up to 13,000

7

feet and formed a perfect backdrop for the delightful green of the valley.

He swung away to the right from the Snake River and continued another few miles to the little town of Jackson. He'd heard the area referred to as Jackson Hole, and that the entire strip along the high upthrusting Grand Tetons to the west was an actual sink where the ground was dropping away at a slow rate. In a few million years, there probably would be a huge lake along the whole rim of the Tetons.

The town looked as if it might have 300 residents. Buckskin couldn't figure out why. It had a stage line, and a few ranches, but nothing else to attract settlers. The valley floor was mostly grazed. He saw a few small parcels that had been cultivated near the river where they probably used ditch irrigation.

Why was there a town here? He didn't wait for an answer. The Grand Teton Cafe showed on his right. It had two buggies, a wagon and six horses outside, so Buckskin figured it must be a good place to eat.

He fingered the quarter in his pocket. It was the last money he had in the whole world. He snorted and walked in as if he was the king of Prussia. He sat down at a table for two and looked at the menu chalked on a board over the counter.

A man wearing a white apron came from the rear with a pad of paper and a pencil. "What'll it be this afternoon?" the man asked. He was in his forties, with a bald pate that had struggling wisps of hair all around his head. His dark eyes critically watched Buckskin, then he glanced at Buckskin's soft hands. The man was about five-ten, with a sallow, indoors complexion, most of his teeth, sharp brown eyes and a start of a bulging gut from his own good food. His hands were clean and strong, leading to firm arms and a strong pair of shoulders.

When Buckskin didn't respond with an order, the man nodded. "I've got a good beef stew today, fresh made this morning with plenty of vegetables in it. Or we have some fine steaks I cut out this afternoon."

"I'll take the steak dinner," Buckskin said.

"That's ninety-five cents," the man said.

"Same way I read it," Buckskin said with a grin. "Make that steak rare. I want it to bleed when I cut into it."

The man hesitated, then nodded and hurried behind the counter and into what Buckskin guessed was the kitchen.

Ten minutes later he came back with two plates. One held an inch-thick steak that covered the china from edge to edge. The other one had four kinds of vegetables and potatoes with gravy.

The middle-aged cafe man held the plates and looked at Buckskin. "First, let's settle an argument. Watched you get off your mount and walk in here. Friend of mine said you're a gunman, with that holster tied down low on your leg. Is he right? Are you a man who makes a living with his iron?"

Buckskin smelled the steak and he wanted it. He shrugged. "I've been known to use my weapon from time to time. I'm no outlaw, but I'm damn hungry."

"I figured. You got the dollar to pay for the meal?" The cafe man still held the plates in his hands.

Buckskin scowled, blew out a lungful of air and stared hard at the man. "Fact is, I don't. I'll work off the dollar."

"You ain't no cowboy, either. No rope burns on your hands and your face ain't sunburned enough. I reckon you can work off the bill."

He set down the plates and silverware, then went for the coffee pot. He poured a steaming cup full and put the pot on a pad at the edge of the table.

The man turned around a chair and sat on it, leaning his chin on his arms across the back of the chair. "My name's Josh Baines. I run this place. Also, I have a problem. A week ago my brother was murdered. I been haranguing the sheriff to find out who done it and he tells me he has no suspects, no evidence, no way of telling who killed my only brother."

"Sounds like somebody got away with murder."

"Not yet, they haven't. I need a man with a gun to help me. I aim to find the killer myself. I knew Elwood better'n anybody in the county. Got me some ideas. I'm no good with weapons, never have been. I need a gunhand to back up my play."

Buckskin cut off another chunk of the blood-red steak and put it in his mouth. When he had it chewed and swallowed, he looked up at Baines.

"You just need a gunhand? Why not hire a detective, somebody who knows how to dig into a case and ferret out the killer?"

"Now who would send a man way out here into nowhere? Not Pinkerton, for damned sure. Anyway, I couldn't afford them. Maybe there's an agency in Cheyenne, but that's three days away even using the train."

Buckskin kept eating. The meal was good, he could stand some regular eating for a time. "How did your brother die, Mr. Baines?"

"Not exactly sure. Turns out he was shot in the legs with a shotgun. That alone would have made him bleed to death. Then somebody put a heavy round into the back of his head. Some cowhands found him out at the edge of town in his buggy. He had a crippled leg and didn't ride much anymore. You interested in helping me?"

"Just as a gun hand?"

"Right. I can do the investigating."

"If the food is always this good, I'll sign on with you."

"Good. Let me tell you a little about my late brother. He was four-inches taller and two years older than me. He came into this country fifteen years ago driving a starter herd of cattle and when he died he had the biggest producing ranch in half the state of Wyoming.

"His ranch is the Box B. Covers more than half of the Snake River Valley through here, extending up twenty, thirty miles to the north. He usually has about 7,000 head of cattle he works. Drives the market-ready steers down to the rail siding at Rock Springs which is about a hundred and eighty miles south and east a bit."

"Has there been a range war going on?" Buckskin asked.

"No. Oh, there was some bad blood between Elwood and the other big rancher up farther north and his Slash S outfit. But never has been any killing. Boundary disputes, water rights, things like that."

Buckskin finished the meal and leaned back. He took a card from his wallet and handed it to the cafe owner. It read:

"Buckskin Lee Morgan. Investigations. Business, Personal, Range. General Delivery, Denver, Colorado."

Josh Baines read the card, turned it over and then read it again. He looked up at Buckskin and grinned. "Young man, looks like you talked yourself into a job right here in Jackson. How much do you charge?"

They soon made an agreement: three dollars a day, a minimum of fifty plus expenses, and a twenty-dollar advance against expenses.

Buckskin shook Baines' hand. "I'll want to know a lot more about your brother. Family, friends, hobbies, groups he belonged to, everything. First, I want to get a hotel room, take a long hot bath and then talk to the undertaker. Oh, is there a sheriff in town? Is this a county seat?"

"Indeed, Teton County."

"Who is the sheriff? Is he a lawman or a desk politician? Is he honest or is he owned by someone?"

Josh Baines snorted. "Sheriff Fillmore Jefferson is a disgrace to the lawmans' profession. He's inept, too fat to ride a horse, vain, underpaid, has only three deputies to cover the whole county, and he'd rather eat than even try to find an outlaw or a killer."

Buckskin laughed. "That paints a fine picture of the man. I'll be back here to see you after I get cleaned up and change clothes." He grinned. "Good doing business with you, Mr. Baines."

Buckskin followed the cafe man to the counter, where he took out twenty dollars in paper money and handed it to Buckskin.

He left the eatery, went across the street to the larger of two hotels he could see, registered and asked for room 212 front.

"Bath tub?" he asked.

"Bathroom on the second floor end of the hall," the room clerk said. "I'll have a boy bring up hot water. Costs twenty-five cents for the hot water. Towels are free."

The five pails of hot water were scalding, and Buckskin cut them with one of cold. He sat in the hot water soaking, and shaved first. It was his first shave in a week and the hot water helped reduce the pain. One of these days he was going to grow a full beard and not worry about shaving.

He scrubbed and washed off and scrubbed again. Each time he took off another layer of trail dust and dirt. After the third time he got down to skin and called it quits. Twice he washed his hair and then stepped out of the tub and reached for his towel.

At the same time, the bathroom door opened and a young woman walked in carrying a stack of white towels. She stopped when she saw him standing there naked. Buckskin didn't bother to cover his crotch.

The girl grinned. "Oh, I thought you were gone. You forgot to lock the door."

"I locked it," Buckskin said.

She laughed. "Yeah. Mind?"

"Not at all. Later tonight? Room 212."

"I knew that. My name's Tilly." She unbuttoned the white blouse she wore and held the cloth back,

13

showing him her breasts. They were large and heavily nippled with small pink areolas.

"A fine set of Grand Tetons," Buckskin said. "Keep them warm for me. I'll be in my room by nine."

"I'll be waiting for you." She buttoned her blouse, then left as quickly as she had come in, taking the towels with her and locking the door behind her with her master key.

Twenty minutes later, Buckskin had dressed in his town clothes: blue wool trousers, a blue and white yoked shirt and his black leather vest. He set the brown Stetson with the flat brim and low crown on his head at the right angle. It had a series of red diamonds on a black headband that circled the hat.

His first call was at the undertaker. The man was short and heavy, with a fat, red-cheeked face. He grinned and pushed out his hand like a medicine show barker. "My name is Horatio Weaver. And I'm in a grave business here. Anything that I can undertake for you I will. Why don't we plot out your problem right now."

"Mr. Weaver, week or so ago you had a customer named Elwood Baines. What do you remember about the condition of the body?"

"Baines. You bet I remember him. You're new in town, why do you want to know?"

"I've been hired by his brother to bring his killers to justice. Can you help me?"

"Not a lot to help. The man was murdered for sure. A whole casket of reasons point to it. That shotgun blast with bird shot from less than ten-feet would have made him bleed to death in half an hour. Then, the bullet shot into the back of his head came before he was dead because the wound bled. See, a body doesn't bleed after it's dead. No pump to force the blood through the tubes, no blood pressure, so no bleeding.

"Well, there could be a little gravity bleeding. Say a man is slashed on his chest, falls on his face and dies. The wound could bleed as blood runs downward and some comes out the wound."

"I understand. Were there any other problems with the body?"

"How the hell did you know? The lips were blue and puffy. I only seen that twice before. Both cases kids got into rat poison and killed themselves. I'm certain that somebody poisoned Elwood Baines. I figure he was coming to see the doctor when he got that final slug in the back of the head."

"Poison. Interesting. I'd guess almost anybody can get rat poison around here?"

"Right down at the general store. Buy enough to kill half the town for fifty-cents."

"I'll bet. Anything else?"

The chunky undertaker scowled and walked away from Buckskin. When he came back he shrugged. "Hell, guess I need to tell somebody. I never even told the family. When I got the body it was fully clothed. I put on the new suit his brother brought down, and when I undressed old Elwood, I was astounded. Somebody had hacked off both his balls. Looked like they done it with a rusty knife. His long underwear was all bloody, but the wound itself had clotted so no telling how long before he died that it happened."

Buckskin rubbed his jaw. "That so. Have there been any reports of rapes in town lately? Or any women complaining about some man being a real cock hound?"

The undertaker half closed his eyes as he evidently thought back a time, then he lifted his brows and shook his head. "None that I can remember. You can check the *Jackson Hole Tribune*. Been anything like that it'd show up there."

When Buckskin thanked the round faced undertaker, the chubby man looked worried. "Mr. Morgan, I'd appreciate it if you kept that confidential about Baines being castrated. I figured no sense bringing up anything that would embarrass the family. He was an important man in this county. Owned the stage line and freight line from here to Rock Springs and a couple of businesses, from what I hear. No sense getting anybody riled up about this."

"I won't reveal it unless it's necessary to trap the killer," Buckskin said. "Thanks again."

Buckskin looked for the courthouse. It was a small frame building on a full sized city block that was mostly vacant and ready for a new, permanent building. He found the sheriff's office and walked in.

A deputy sheriff sat at a desk and looked up and waved. "Be with you in a minute," he said and went back to writing on a card on his desk. A moment later he came forward. He wore jeans and a blue shirt with a tan leather vest over it and a six-gun in leather on his hip.

"Yes, sir, what can I do for you this afternoon?"

"Looking for Sheriff Jefferson. Lee Morgan is my name."

The name meant nothing to the deputy. Buckskin figured this was a good sign.

"Yes, sir. I'll see if the Sheriff is busy. Just a minute."

He gave Buckskin one more long look before going to the back of the 15-foot-long office. He knocked on a door and then entered to the room beyond. He was back in the time it takes to turn around a mule team.

"Sheriff Jefferson says to come right in. He has a busy morning but if it won't take too long, he'll be proud to talk to you."

Buckskin had his red diamond hat in his hand as he went through the door the deputy indicated. The office was typical. United States flag on the wall, map of the county on the other wall, big desk made of oak, and a short and heavy man sitting behind it wearing a high crowned white Stetson with a wide brim turned up on both sides. He looked up out of dark eyes.

"What can I do for you, Morgan?"

Buckskin handed the sheriff a card and started talking before the sheriff could.

"I'm here working for Josh Baines. I'm hunting the person or persons who killed Elwood Baines."

"So is this office. That case is still open."

"Then we can work together."

"I did my work, you're welcome to do yours."

"I'd like to see any files, reports, information that you have on the case to give me some background."

The sheriff stared over wire rimmed glasses for a minute, then he shrugged. "Fine. You won't find anything more than we did which was buffalo squat. My clerk will get you the file."

The sheriff turned and bellowed toward the door. "Larson, get in here."

A short time later Buckskin Morgan sat at an empty desk in the front office looking over the written reports and information on the death of Elwood Baines.

The entire file consisted of a duplicate of the death certificate, a sketchy report by a Deputy Larson who was the lawman on the scene, and a one paragraph report later by Sheriff Jefferson that the investigation had been completed and there was no evidence of who the killer or killers were.

"This is it?" Buckskin asked Deputy Larson.

"Yep. I was out at the death site myself. Not a chance to find out who gunned him. No evidence, no witnesses. What the hell can we do, make up something?"

"How long did you investigate the case?"

The deputy pushed back his white, high crowned hat which must be the county sheriff's uniform headgear. "Damn, I figure that I put more than a full day in talking to people. Just gave up."

Buckskin nodded and went back to the report. He read over the hand-printed one again:

Body of Elwood Baines, local rancher and businessman, found dead in his buggy on north road a hundred-yards from the Barrett place. We received a complaint about a horse making a lot of noise. Found the subject fallen to the side in the buggy. Legs wrapped up due to previous shotgun wounds. Single bullet in back of his head probably caused death.

Spoke to family, business associates, townspeople. No one came under suspicion, nobody

18

gave any reason someone would want to kill the man. With no motive and no suspects, the case has been put in the unsolved file.

Buckskin thanked the deputy, gave him the file, and left. At least the sheriff didn't know about the castration or the possibility of poisoning. So far those were the best clues that he had. He would earn his money on this case. He headed back toward the cafe. There had to be dozens of vital facts he didn't know about this man yet or about the situation here. The best place to start was with the deceased's brother, Josh Baines.

# Chapter Two

Buckskin walked into the Grand Teton Cafe and sat down on the end stool near the kitchen. The owner was there with a cup of coffee before the big detective had settled in.

"Need to talk to you," Buckskin said. "I need to know everything you know about your brother from day one."

"Supper rush coming up," Josh Baines said. He shrugged. "Come on back. I can talk while I cook."

Buckskin found a wall to lean against just beyond the big stove with twelve removable lids. It was the largest wood fired cook stove he'd ever seen.

"Tell me what your brother owned in the county and how much he was worth."

Josh looked at an order stub pushed under a rubber band on a drum that rotated and could be read from the front of the cafe or the kitchen. He read off an order, scooped a big bowl of beef stew out of a heavy metal cooker, put it on a plate and pushed it across a small chin level shelf that extended into the front of the eatery.

"What's he worth? Was worth, you mean. Start with the Box B ranch. He turned an Englishman down who offered him two-hundred and fifty-thousand dollars last year for the ranch. The steers, brood cows and bulls on the place are worth a lot more than that. I'd put the ranch value at about three-hundred and fifty-thousand."

Josh looked at another order and kept his hands busy. "Then there's the stage and freight lines. Not big money makers, but Elwood liked to think of it more as a service for the people here in Jackson. His lawyer said the two together were valued at a little over twenty-thousand."

"Heard he owned some businesses in town," Buckskin said.

"True. Just which ones, I'm not sure. You'll have to talk to his lawyer, a man by the name of Adler Pickering. He's got a list of the estate, and a copy of the last will. It was read three days ago. I wasn't mentioned. Elwood thought I was wasting my time cooking. I love to cook. If I make a living at it, fine. If not, I'll do something else for cash money and cook for pleasure."

"You expected to be left out of the will?"

"Knew for certain. I was one of the witnesses when he drew up his last will and Pickering had me over to his office to sign it. Elwood said I didn't have any need for money, so he wouldn't will me any.

Oh, his lawyer got five-thousand as the executor of his estate."

"Who got the estate?"

"His widow, son and daughter."

"How old are the kids?"

"Elwood got a late start on his family. His wife, Raquel, is only thirty-eight now. Kenny is sixteen and Midge is fifteen. Good kids."

"They live at the ranch, I'd guess. Where is it?"

"Only three miles out of town. Kids came to school every day. Kenny is a top cowhand already. Midge is small and frail, like her ma. Writes poetry."

"So that should eliminate you as a suspect," Buckskin said.

"Me a suspect?"

"I consider everyone the killer until I eliminate that person. Who do you think killed your brother?"

"Don't know. Midge told me her father was in good health when he left the ranch to come to town to check the mail. He was expecting an important letter from Chicago."

"Did the important letter come?" Buckskin asked.

"Don't know. They might not even have picked up the mail yet. It's been a tough week for the family. All of the family."

"Who were your brother's enemies?"

"Write out a list. Half the county hated him because he was a rich, self-made man. The other half hated him because they couldn't do the same thing."

"You said you had some ideas when we first talked. Want to share them with me?"

Josh flipped a man sized steak on the grill and looked back at Buckskin. "I'd heard he had some woman trouble, like he got some girl in a family way."

"Here in town?"

"Yes. Not a pretty thing to dig into. Then there's one other problem that don't set right with me."

"Such as?"

"For the past ten years various groups have been trying to get a spur rail line up to Jackson. Claim it will make the town boom. Bring in settlers, be a way to ship out timber from the mountains and any mining ore or coal we can locate. Nothing much ever happened.

"Then six months ago a new wave of speculation hit the town. Various well-dressed men visited Jackson, looked around, stayed at the hotel a night or two and took the stage back to Rock Springs. Almost always Elwood squired the gents around, took them to dinner, made sure they had what they wanted, then waved goodbye to them the next day on the stage."

"What seems wrong about that?" Spur asked.

"Not legally wrong, just financially. Elwood didn't have the kind of money it takes to put in a hundred and eighty miles of track. I know, I know about the railroad land grants the federal government gives the railroad builders. They get ten sections of land on alternate miles along the track laid, and work trains moving over it for each mile of track.

"That much land between here and Rock Springs would be worth hundreds of millions of dollars. But laying track costs big money, too. Some say ten-thousand dollars a mile on the straight and level. Get into the mountains with cuts and fills and trestles and the price can go up to sixty, seventy-thousand a mile."

# Kit Dalton

Buckskin pushed his hat back on his head. "True, but think how much a hundred and eighty miles of track, times ten sections a mile, is going to be worth to the railroad builder. That's a thousand and eight-hundred square miles of land. That's more than a million acres."

"I can't think figures that big," Josh said. He flipped another steak on the grill and Buckskin's mouth watered.

"Fry me up one of them, Josh. Just seer it on both sides and leave me some chewing time in the middle."

Buckskin thought over what he'd learned about the victim. Fast man with a dollar. What was the important letter from Chicago? Some go-ahead from a financial backer for the railroad spur line to Jackson? Buckskin finished his meal and went outside to walk it off. He strolled past the newspaper: the *Jackson Hole Tribune*. The door was open to the small office.

Inside, Buckskin talked with a slender man wearing a green eye shade. He was about sixty with a full white beard, eyeglasses and a running nose that kept his white handkerchief poised in one hand.

"Rape?" The newsman grinned. "This isn't Chicago or New York or even St. Louis. Far as I know there never has been a rape reported in Jackson since I been here, going on fifteen years now."

"Indeed, a lucky place to live," Buckskin said. "Oh, have any young ladies from town gone away to school or to visit a relative for an extended length of time?"

"You imply that they have gone away to have a baby. No, I can't think of any. Now and then a young

24

woman does leave town, but I can't remember any who came back with a child or rumors that she had birthed while away. Don't remember a single one."

"Just wondering," Buckskin said. Then he told the newsman about his quest to find out who murdered the county's leading citizen.

"I wish you good luck. I dug into it a little, but just nothing there, not a single clue did I find. I'd give it a guess. This wasn't any spur of the moment killing. Somebody planned it out carefully, probably laid in wait somewhere between his ranch and town, and did him in proper."

"Why the shotgun and then a six-gun slug behind the head?" Buckskin asked.

"Oh, to be sure of the kill, I'd say."

"Same person?"

The newsman frowned, looked up and wet his lips and stared hard at Buckskin. "You don't let go, do you? I see what you mean. A man carrying a shotgun to do in a gent in a buggy, wouldn't be likely to pack a six-gun shooter as well."

"Any sign of buckshot on the buggy?" Buckskin asked.

The newsman wiped a hand across his face. "Never thought to take a look special. I sure didn't see any damage to it remembering back. No, sir. Elwood Baines had to be shot somewhere else out of the buggy. Then he got in and raced for town and the doctor. Only somebody stopped him with that slug in his brain."

"Looks that way," Buckskin said. "So could be one man, could be two shooters. Maybe two men killed Elwood Baines."

The newsman told Buckskin his name was Whit Forsythe. "I think you may be on to something there, young man. You come in any time and talk about the killing. I'll keep an open mind and lend some help when I can. I know a few more folks in town than you do."

"Good, Whit. What about the railroad rumor?"

"You've heard that already? Nobody knows a damn thing. I couldn't get none of them fancy dressed gents to give me the time of day on their expensive gold-filled watches. Something was happening. It just smelled like a railroad deal. A spur line up here from Rock Springs. Take out lumber, maybe some coal or some gold or silver ore, who knows what we might find. Ain't heard hide nor brisket of it since Elwood died."

"So you think he was in on it?"

"Had to be, one way or the other. Don't see how he could have that much money. Maybe he was the local contact for some combine of financial men."

"Any locals who didn't like the idea of the steel rails coming to town?" Buckskin asked.

"Not that I heard about. You best take a copy of last week's edition and read up on Jackson. Good way to get acquainted."

"I can see you're busy. This press day?"

"Press night, once I get this final story for page one done. Read about it tomorrow."

Buckskin thanked the newsman and walked out to the dusk of the Jackson, Wyoming evening. The little town rested in the hollow below the Grand Tetons but still over six-thousand two-hundred feet in the air. There would be a chill to the air even on the warmest summer night. He watched lights blossom in the houses and a few stores.

He was getting a feel for the small village, and learning about the rich man who got himself killed by one, two, three or maybe even four people. Buckskin knew that one person could not do so much damage to the body by him or herself. He'd seen a few women killers in his days. Most of them were far more vicious and angry than men who killed.

Who had killed Elwood Baines?

He had his choice of what actually killed the man: poison, castration, shotgun at the legs, or the large caliber round into the back of his head. His guess would be the poisoning took place first but took some hours to kill. The shotgun might have come next. Baines could have headed for the doctor's office when the gunman came and put a round in the back of his head. Even after that, someone could have castrated the man.

No, the bleeding. The castration had to come before the fatal blast from the .44 six-gun.

Buckskin shook his head. Things were going in a whirl. Never had he seen such a variety of deadly means employed against one corpse. It didn't even really matter which method killed the man, any one of them could have.

He'd seen a man bleed to death from an impromptu castration once. He thought about the chopped off testicles. Unusual to say the least. An angry father?

Tilly! Yes. The maid at the hotel looked to be an age where she would know the female gossip around town. In a place this small a lot of people would surely know if one of the girls or single women became pregnant out of wedlock. He turned toward the hotel.

It wasn't seven o'clock yet. Maybe Tilly would be early.

Buckskin moved along the boardwalk like some big cat stalking its prey. He was six-feet tall and 175 pounds, with blondish-brown hair and brown eyes. He had a strong mouth, square-cut chin, and wide-set eyes that had backed down many a want-to-be gunman with their deadly gaze. Those same eyes could mellow and melt the heart of a pretty girl. Women usually were attracted to his rugged good looks, and Buckskin was not one to be stingy with his affection.

He walked to the hotel and went up the stairs without a pause. Buckskin came to his room on silent feet, gently turned the knob at 212 and found the door unlocked. He had his six-gun out and cocked as he pushed the door open hard so it swung around and hit the wall behind it. Only then did he look around the jamb into the room.

Tilly sat on the edge of the bed. Her blouse was off and one hand massaged a breast. She looked up and smiled. "Come on in, Mr. Lee Morgan. I promise not to bite—unless you want me to."

Buckskin grinned and went into the room, closed the door and locked it, then took the straight-backed chair and pushed the back of it under the doorknob so it rested on the rear two legs. To come into the room, a person would have to smash the sturdy chair.

He walked over to Tilly who stood up to greet him. The top of her head came to his chin. She was five-two, with dark hair that flowed around her shoulders and was cut in flat bangs straight across her forehead. She hugged Buckskin and pulled him down on the bed to sit beside her.

"What took you so long? I've been waiting since six o'clock."

"I see you started without me."

"Just a warm-up so I'll be ready for you." She kissed him and put one of his hands on her breasts. "Feel me good. They been just aching for your hands on them ever since they said hello this afternoon."

She kissed him again and one hand went to his crotch where she found the start of his erection. Her hand knew just where and how to rub to encourage him.

Buckskin pushed back from her and caught both her hands. "First, some business. How old are you?"

"Almost eighteen, and I finished school."

"Good, you know most of the girls your age and a little younger and older in town?"

"Most of them. Ain't all that many."

"You know the ones who fuck around?"

She grinned. "Now why you asking me that? Ain't I gonna be enough for your big whanger?"

"You'll be plenty. I'm interested to find out if any of the young girls in town is pregnant or became pregnant in the last month or two."

"Lordy, you're an out-of-towner, ain't you? Most of the girls know something like that. It just gets out. Two dumb girls got themselves knocked up within the last month. Elly, a pretty one, done got herself promised already. She picked the guy who had poked her who she liked best and told everybody he was the pappy. He said he'd marry her right away."

"What about the other one?"

"I can't find out who she is. Certain she ain't gonna get married or I'd hear about it. I got ears all over this town when it comes to sexy stuff."

"I need to know. Can you find out for me who the other pregnant girl is? Tell you what: I'll keep you well poked while I'm in town. You come up with a name for me and we'll make love until we're both so tired we can't pop."

"Deal, deal! Oh, damn but this is my lucky day. I'll keep your old dong so tired he won't want to look my crotch in the eye. Sort of. I got me a couple of ideas who the pregnant bitch is, but I'll have to check it out more. In the meantime. . . ."

She pushed him down on the bed and lay beside him, her hand at his crotch again. Her other hand unbuttoned his vest and shirt and toyed with the dark hair on his chest.

"Jeeze but I love a man with a hairy chest. How we going to make love the first time?"

"Any way you want."

"Great, me on top."

She sat up then and undressed him, boots first, then socks and shirt and pants. When she stripped down his underwear she whistled in delight.

"Whoee! Look at that whanger. Must be a foot long. Let me get the rest of my clothes off!"

She stripped naked, rolled on the bed, pushed him on his back and crawled on top of him. For a moment she lay there flat on top, her breasts hard against his bare chest, her hips grinding slowly against him, exciting his erection further.

She leaned up on her hands so she could see his face. "You really let me be on top?"

"Sure. Can you make it up there?"

"Hell, I can cum in any of about fifty different positions. Not all of them in one night, I'd guess." Her breasts jiggled as she moved and the drooping mounds delighted Buckskin. He reached up and licked one breast, then bit gently on her nipple.

"Oh, damn, do that again and I'll cum before you get inside me."

He moved to the other nipple and licked it, bit and then chewed on her mounds until she began to pant and her hips rotated on his. Then she stormed into a climax that shook her like a grouse in a retriever's jaws. Tilly rumbled and bleated. She gasped and her whole body spasmed as if she were having a seizure. Then she wailed and crooned and her hips pounded downward against him a dozen more times before she shrieked high and soft and plaintively until she tapered off and collapsed on top of him, panting and crying softly with the force of it.

Five minutes later she lifted away from him and moved down, still over his naked form. She pushed his legs together, spread her legs outside of his and then moved her crotch slowly toward his erection. Her hand lifted him, angled him just right as she lowered onto his lance like a trusty sheath and moaned with a wild urgency as she sank down and down until their pelvic bones meshed together and she could go no farther.

Her eyes widened and she stared at him. "Great Aunt Thursday, but you got one long pecker. I don't think I ever felt nobody push that far into my little twat before. Swear you're halfway into my chest by now. Don't move, not for a minute. This big long dick of yours is going to take some getting used to."

Buckskin lay there fondling her breasts, making her nipples surge and pulse and fill again with hot blood.

Slowly she began to move in a half circle with her hips, then back. After a half dozen of those she lifted off him an inch and dropped back down. A low moan escaped from her tightly closed lips. She tried it again four-inches up his shaft and got the same kind of reaction.

Buckskin began to thrust upward to meet her and in a few minutes they had a rhythm worked out that delighted her and moved him down the road to the glory land. She established a rocking forward and back motion as well as up and down and Buckskin followed her lead. Soon both of them were panting and Buckskin knew that he couldn't hold out much longer.

Tilly screeched in wonder and delight as a new climax tore through her. That triggered Buckskin who exploded in her and rammed her bare little bottom two-feet off the bed before he let her come back down. He made the same move eight times, then settled into the mattress with her body still spasming and shaking and rattling like an empty boxcar on an uneven roadbed.

She at last settled down and kissed him and fell flat on top of his naked body with closed eyes.

"Nap time," she said.

Buckskin lay there thinking it through. If Tilly could tell him who the pregnant girl was, he could

have a lead to one person who hurt Baines, and might
have seen someone else at or near the death scene.

He relaxed, trying to come up with a plan for tomorrow. He didn't. The woman moved beside him and he
knew he had an all night party. He'd work out his
agenda in the morning. Right now he had far more
urgent matters to attend to.

He rolled Tilly over and caught both her breasts.
"Next time it's my choice of positions," he said.

Tilly grinned and nodded. "Damn, I hope you're
good for at least five times tonight."

Buckskin was.

# Chapter Three

The next morning, when Buckskin woke up at six-thirty on schedule, Tilly was gone. He nodded. Good. No clinging-vine chatter, no promises, no lies, no commitments.

He had breakfast at the Grand Teton Cafe where he talked with Josh Baines.

"Getting my feet on the ground," Buckskin said. "Getting some facts lined up and trying to figure out who some reasonable suspects might be."

"I can't help you much there."

"I'm going out to the ranch this morning to talk to the widow, the kids and some of the hands. They might know something they haven't told anyone. Happens."

He had a big breakfast and talked with Josh for another ten minutes in the kitchen, but Josh couldn't remember any more about his big brother's actions and enemies than he had the day before.

Buckskin rented a horse at the livery and an hour later he rode up to the home place ranch buildings of the Box B spread. There were more than a dozen structures, from two large barns and a two-story ranch house, to out buildings and a well house.

A cowboy eased out of a bunkhouse and met Buck as he stepped down from the mount.

"Morning. I'm looking for Mrs. Baines."

"She ain't hiring."

"Fine, I'm not looking for work. She in the house?"

The back screen door slammed as a woman stepped outside from what Buck figured was the kitchen. She held a cup of coffee in one hand and squinted into the sun at them.

"Who is it, Rayford?"

"Didn't say. Wants to see you."

"Send him up."

Buckskin turned, left his mount ground tied and walked the short way to the Widow Baines. She was pale, thin; nervous eyes watched him approach. Her right hand caressed the coffee cup, then dropped to her side, then lifted back to the cup. She moved her hand to her dark hair and touched the strands that had slipped out from a bun at the back of her neck.

"Mrs. Baines?"

"Yes."

"I'm Buckskin Lee Morgan. I'm a detective trying to find out what happened to your husband."

"I didn't hire any detective."

"True, I'm working for your brother-in-law Josh Baines. He figures it's about time to get to the bottom of how and why your husband died. I figured you wouldn't object to that."

She withdrew a half step; her whole body looked as if it had shrunken an inch and lost twenty pounds in a second. Then her face tried to recover and she nodded, with the semblance of a smile. "Do tell. Josh always was a plodder. Now he's plodding into this. It's none of his business, but I, too, would like to know who shot my husband. Can you really find out what happened after two weeks?"

"That's what I plan on doing. Would it be better if we talked inside? The hot sun must not be good for your light complexion."

She smiled for a fraction of a second and Buckskin saw where there once had been beauty. Now it looked pasted over by endless days of worry, trouble and death.

She held out a hand tentatively, as if wondering if he would shake it or slice it off at her wrist. "I'm Raquel Baines. Please come into the kitchen. Would you like a cup of coffee? It's fresh boiled."

A few minutes later, Buckskin sipped the hot brew that was strong enough to float an iron hulled steamship.

"So what you're saying is that your husband was in good spirits and good health when he left the house shortly after dinner the day he died."

"Yes. He said he had some business in town. Elwood often drove into town to play cards and to have a drink or two. We didn't have much of a real marriage." She looked away, then back at him. "We've slept in separate bedrooms for over eight years now."

Buckskin noted that interesting fact, but moved on. "Did your husband mention anyone he was going to meet or to see that evening? A business deal, something about ranch supplies, one of his business managers?"

Mrs. Baines pulled back into her frail body again. It was as if she actually became smaller, more insignificant. She shook her head.

"Elwood didn't talk to me much lately. He didn't say a single word that night about what he was going to do in town or who he might see. Sorry I can't help you there. I only wish that I could."

"How long were you married?"

"Eighteen years come a week from Thursday." She cocked her head to one side, her fingers covering her mouth for a moment. "Mr. Morgan, how much is Josh paying you?"

"Three dollars a day plus expenses."

"Fiddlesticks. How can he expect to hire competent people for that kind of a wage? I'm interested in knowing who shot my husband, Mr. Morgan. When you find out, I'll pay you five-thousand dollars, whether the person who did it is dead or alive, whether he's prosecuted for murder or not. I simply must know who shot my husband."

"Generous. But why would you do that? I'll do my best work for Josh for three dollars a day. Why a new offer?"

"To urge you on and to be sure that you find the villain." Her eyes glowed with an intensity he didn't think the slight woman possessed. She nodded mostly to herself. "Yes, I must know who shot my husband."

"He was shot twice, you know."

"The round in the back of his head. I want to know who fired that fatal shot."

"I'll know before this case is finished, Mrs. Baines, you can be sure of that. Now, I'd like to meet your children. Are they at home?"

When the woman went to the stairs and called, a girl of fifteen came down the steps. She was a copy of her mother. Smaller, yet with larger breasts, more substance to her young body but with a face nearly identical to that of her mother. A curiously small nose, dark brown eyes with long lashes. Her brunette hair came down over her shoulders flowing sleek and well combed. She was an inch shorter than her mother's five-two, but she would be two inches taller than her mother when she finished growing.

"Mr. Morgan, I'd like you to meet Midge, our— my daughter. Midge is our bookworm. Midge, this is the detective we've heard about in town."

Midge stiffened momentarily, then moved her shoulders, unfreezing her whole body. She stepped forward and held out her delicate hand with long, thin fingers.

"I've heard someone was in town asking a lot of questions. We want to know who killed father, of course, but we don't want to have to relive those bad times. I'm sure you understand."

"Oh, I do, Midge. However, sometimes bad memories can help us understand just what happened and who was responsible. Did you see your father that evening before he left for town?"

"At dinner, then again before he drove off."

"How did he seem? Was he angry or happy."

"I didn't notice. At dinner he was charming. When I saw him last he was in the buggy and looked more serious, even a little grim."

"Do you know who he was going to town to see?"

"No. I don't know much about his business affairs."

Buckskin thanked her, and the widow invited him outside to meet her son, Kenny. He was already a top cowboy and was doing a lot of the work in running the huge cattle side of the ranch.

The widow had been a zero when it came to helping him with his search, and the daughter dropped that figure even lower. There was little help here.

They found the young Kenny Baines in the large corral where two men were breaking horses. The kid was sixteen, lean and tanned, with a working cowboy hat that showed plenty of sweat and dust stains. He leaned down from his mount and shook hands with Buckskin.

"Howdy, Mr. Morgan. Sure hope you can find the man who murdered my pa. If'n you can't, reckon I'll have to. Ma says she won't let me go, she needs me here, but a man can't let something like this pass and just not do anything about it. I bet you understand about that."

"You're right, Kenny. Looks like you've got your hands full right here with the ranch. Why don't you give me a couple of weeks to try to track down the culprits. If I can't find them, I'll turn over the job to you. Fair enough?"

"Yeah, Mr. Morgan. Fair enough. I hold you to that."

Buckskin saw a flash of gratitude from the Widow Baines, then the expression vanished and her frown returned. Mrs. Baines nodded at her son and he waved and rode back to the horse in the middle of the corral.

"You'll be going then, Mr. Morgan?" the widow asked.

"That I will, Mrs. Baines. I thank you for the coffee and for your frank and honest briefing about your late husband. Oh, a question. Do you think your husband was involved in some business deal in town that might have made him an enemy angry enough to do what happened?"

The thin woman thought about it a moment, waved him forward toward his horse and talked as they walked.

"No. I don't think so. Frankly I didn't know enough about the business firms that my late husband owned in town. I'm finding out now. I'll handle running those and help Kenny with the ranch. Eventually, he'll take over the ranch all by himself.

"What I know of the operations in town shows that he hired men to manage the stores for him, held total control, but did not step on enough of the local merchants' toes to bring down their wrath. He didn't force other stores out of business if that's what you're driving at."

He thanked her, stepped into his saddle and turned his horse north. Midge came out the kitchen door and waved at him. There was something about the way she stood that triggered a memory and it took him a few moments to make the connection.

Then he made the connection and he chuckled. It had been when he was in Abilene and met that little dark eyed whore. She had a body about the same as Midge's and she loved to stand the same way, a sassy, here-it-is-boys-but-you-got-to-pay-to-see-it-unwrapped kind of posture.

Buckskin shook his head. Midge was only fifteen. Comparing her to the whore in Abilene was only a fleeting thought. Still, there was something essentially sexual about the young ranch girl. Was she a sex bomb waiting for someone to light her fuse? Buckskin figured he would never know, so he turned his horse to the north, followed the Snake as it wound its way toward the other ranch up here, the Slash S brand owned by Lucas Shelby.

It didn't seem reasonable that the rancher would have any hand in Baines's death. However, at this point, Buckskin had to cover every possible suspect. Two big ranchers facing each other and squabbling over water rights and division of spring calves certainly could be a major problem after several years. Things had a way of building.

He came to the smaller Slash S shortly before noon. A fenced lane led into the place. Four buildings had been placed around a one-story ranch house. He saw two hands near the corral. Before he could call to them, a barrel chested man over six feet met Buckskin. The big detective stepped down from the sorrel and nodded at the other man.

"I'm Shelby. You must be that detective guy I heard about was in town asking lots of questions. Come on in and have a home brewed beer. Not cold but we aim to put in an ice house, maybe next winter when we have some spare time. You ever seen an ice house? Love those damn things."

Shelby was a bear of a man with a woolly full beard that showed half gray, lots of dark hair on top and a pair of sparkling green eyes that Buckskin bet never missed a thing.

He led Buckskin onto a screened porch and motioned to a pair of wooden chairs with arm rests.

"Made them myself last winter. I love to work with wood. Rancher's got to do something when the snow flies." A pair of beer bottles sat on the table and he motioned again. "Saw you coming up the lane. Figured you could wet your whistle with a brew. Don't know what the content is, somewhere between four and six percent I'd figure. Got a nice little kick to it. You a beer drinker?"

"From way back. You're right about the detective angle. I'm going to find out who killed Elwood Baines. How can you help me? Did you do it?"

Shelby laughed. "Hell, no. Not that I'm sorry he's gone. I might have done it myself if he kept pushing me another few years." He snapped the tops off both bottles and handed one to Buckskin. They sat in the chairs.

"Elwood lived his whole life by intimidating people. He bluffed and he huffed and he whacked you a good one if you didn't back off after his bluffing. Oh, he wasn't all bluff, but that worked on most folks."

"But not on you, right? How did he whack you?"

"He began to harass me the first day I drove my starter herd into the valley. I knew where his boundaries were, his homesteading boundaries. Rest was open range. I had pounded my stakes and angled my homestead a hundred-yards wide and in hundred-yard long shots upstream on the Snake. That way I homesteaded nearly six miles of river frontage.

"Three Box B riders ordered us off *their* range. I showed them my homesteading papers all legal and right and the riders backed off. Next day Elwood Baines himself came to where we'd pitched two tents and started building a corral. I spotted him coming and we had all ten of us around the spot with rifles loaded and off safety. I positioned the armed men so Baines could see them plainly.

"I showed Baines my homesteading papers and Baines tried to tear them up. I knocked him down and rifle slugs kicked up dirt at Baines' feet and near his two hands. They left screaming threats.

"That same night my starter herd got stampeded with black powder bombs and ran to hell and away. Never did find some of them. So the next night the biggest barn on the Baines place burned to the ground. To this day I wonder about the coincidence of the two bad things happening." His eyes danced.

"Ain't had no real trouble out of Baines since. The man liked to bluff. But when a man called his bluff he'd back down."

"Any big problems between you two in the last month or so?" Buckskin asked.

"Not that you would notice. Some line markers, a few unclaimed spring calves. Hell, we've had a truce and lived under it for eight years. Like I said before, I didn't kill Baines if that's what you're scratching around about. I had no reason to. Anyway, if I'd wanted to kill the man, I'd have done it with a rifle from a hundred yards."

Buckskin tipped the brown beer bottle and drained the last of the brew. "Yes, now that's a sturdy home brew. I appreciate your background about Baines, and your honesty."

"We never got along, but hell, no man deserves to die that way. Shot twice I hear."

"At least." Buckskin stood. "Thanks for your help, I best be getting back to town."

"Long ride without any chow. Almost noon. We feed good here at the Slash S."

After a threshers' noon feast, Buckskin thanked the ranch owner for his hospitality, waved and headed back for town. It was an eighteen mile ride and he didn't know of any shortcuts.

It was after five that afternoon when he turned in his rented horse at the livery at the edge of town and went up to his second floor room. The door was locked. He went in and found a note on the middle of the bed.

"Buck. Sorry I missed you. I got to work tonight. Got me an idea who our pregnant little bitch in heat is. We'll talk later." It was signed Tilly.

# Chapter Four

Buckskin washed up, went down to the hotel eatery for a quick supper and hurried back to his room. He didn't want to miss talking to Tilly again. It looked as if he at last had a lead. The man who castrated Baines could have done that first, watched him suffer, berated him for an hour until the crotch bleeding stopped and then put the six-gun to Baines's head to blow his brains out. Yes. It could have happened that way.

Where the hell was Tilly? He waited in his room until seven o'clock, then went down and paced the lobby until the room clerk asked him if there was a problem. Buckskin started to ask him where Tilly lived, but that would get the girl in trouble with the management. That was the last thing he wanted to happen.

By eight o'clock he was back in his room cleaning

and oiling his Colt .45. When he finished that, he worked over the spare weapon he carried in his kit bag, a deadly little .45 derringer. It was an over and under and had come in handy more than once.

Finally, there was a soft knock on the door.

Tilly stood there in her Sunday-Go-To-Meeting dress and a big grin.

"Told you I was busy, friend of mine got married late this afternoon." Tilly grinned. "Right about now Sue is getting her cute little twat poked for the first time. Damn but I'd like to be there and see how she takes it."

He let her inside and closed the door. She kissed him hard on the mouth, pressing her warm body tightly against his. When she eased away she laughed softly. "Hey, maybe I'll get married someday, who knows. Then I get me a man anytime I want him."

Buckskin caressed her breasts as she thrust them out at him. She looked up and grinned. "Right now in my best dress?"

"Depends on what you have to tell me. Our pregnant little lady?"

"Oh, that. I did some talking around. Three or four of us know most everybody who is getting bedded here in town. It ain't that big a place. Three of us figure it's got to be Irene Tiny Tits Channing. She's wanted it so bad the last three or four months that she'd take on anybody who wore pants. Honest. She was something. Trying to make up for no big mamas up on top I guess."

"Who is Irene Channing?"

"Hey, that's right, you don't know. Irene is the daughter of the preacher here in town. It's nondenominational, which might mean the preacher got booted out of his last church or something. Anyway, Irene is his loose as a goose little girl. Not so little, and she's seventeen.

"We didn't know for sure, but then this afternoon I heard that little sweet Irene is leaving us. She's going to her aunt's house in Omaha to go to school. *Go to school?* They can't be fooling anyone who knows Irene. The only school she'll go to is how to take care of her baby."

Buckskin frowned. "This complicates things. A preacher's brat. That might punch a hole in my theory here."

"Why did you need to know?"

"I'm working on the Baines killing."

"So?"

"So there might be a connection. Might be. I'd much rather Irene wasn't a preacher's kid."

Tilly giggled. "Yeah, about now I'd bet old high and mighty Dwight Channing wishes she wasn't his kid either." Tilly watched him. She reached down and rubbed his crotch, found a growing member there.

"So, does this change things? You have some spare time right now or not?"

She kept rubbing. Buckskin grabbed her hand. "I don't think the best when you're doing that." He grinned and pecked a kiss on her lips. "Tell me, this preacher. Is he a fire and brimstone man, like the Baptists, or more sedate like the Methodists?"

"Somewhere in between. Not the best preacher in the world, I've heard. My mom says he's not dedicated enough, too prone to the ways of the world and the devil."

Buckskin ginned. "What I was waiting to hear." He bent and kissed both her breasts through the dress, then leaned up.

"Tell the girls I can't do better than that for tonight. I've got to go see the preacher."

"I could go along and have him marry us."

"You're not ready yet, Tilly. You're having too much fun fucking around, right?"

She grinned. "Yeah, right. When I get nailed like Irene sweetheart did, then's time enough to start looking for a husband. Probably just latch on to the last one who spread my thighs."

Buckskin put on his hat, checked the six-gun at his belt and herded Tilly toward the door.

"I don't want to go. Just a quick one."

"Not tonight. Business. I've got to tend to business. You're the fun part. Maybe later on tonight."

"Can I stay here?"

"Best not." He edged her out the door and she went down the stairs ahead of him as if by agreement. He waited a bit to put some distance between them. The preacher. He could do the job as well as anyone, depended on the man. Time for a visit.

Buckskin didn't want to risk asking the desk clerk how to find the preacher. Instead he asked two matronly women in front of the hotel. They knew. They told him.

A three block walk later, Buckskin knocked on the door of a small house beside a white painted church with a New England type steeple. He'd only seen them in pictures before.

The man who answered the door appeared to be about forty, Buckskin guessed. Plenty old enough to have a daughter of seventeen.

"Reverend Channing?"

"Yes, what can I do for you?"

"I'm Lee Morgan, in town for a short time. I'm trying to learn more about the rancher Elwood Baines. I understand he was a member of your church."

Channing's eyes widened and he quivered a moment as if he was about to break and run. He beat down what Buckskin figured was raw panic and looked at his caller. Channing was a big man, six-feet even and at least 240 pounds. He had a fat face that was clean shaven and he was balding down a strip in the middle of his head.

"Elwood Baines is dead and buried. Don't you think we should let it stand at that?"

"I'm afraid not, Reverend Channing. The man was murdered. Whoever did the deed is a sinner and a killer and should be brought to justice before the law and before God."

The preacher's face had been tense but somehow passive. Now darting little indentations worked through the stiff exterior. He blinked several times, then bobbed his head.

"Of course. All men are responsible for their actions. I was only thinking of the widow and the two children. They have suffered enough. Any kind of a public trial would be such a terrific strain on the family, especially the widow. . . ."

"How well did you know Mr. Baines?"

"Well, but not on a personal level. He came to services, took part in church activities when he could. He was a rich and extremely busy man."

"You sound as if you didn't like him."

"Not at all. He was busy, didn't take enough time

for church activities." The minister shrugged. "But a lot of men are like that. Can't fault a man for that."

"I'm trying to learn as much about Mr. Baines as I can. You know, his friends, who he liked, who he socialized with, what were his tastes in the pleasures of life."

The minister shook his head. "I'm afraid I'm not the man to talk to. Since I didn't see much of Mr. Baines—" He lifted his hands in a helpless gesture.

"I understand. Seems that Mr. Baines was not a well known man around this town even though he'd lived here for fifteen years."

"Mr. Baines did not have a lot of close friends in town, even though he owned twelve business establishments. Now perhaps some of his problems—" The minister stopped and looked away. "I shouldn't have said that. I'm not one to spread scandal and rumors. I wish you well on your inquiry."

That was when Buckskin realized that they were still standing at the front door. He had not been invited inside. Strange. He touched the brim of his hat, feeling somehow obligated to this religious leader.

"Thank you anyway, Mr. Channing. Thanks for giving me some of your time."

Buckskin turned and walked down the three steps to the path that led out to the street and turned toward the business section of town. On this side street there were no wooden plank walkways, no curbs or hard surfaced streets. Just some surveyor's stakes as a testament to where one property stopped and the next started.

The preacher was indeed curious. At first the man seemed as tight as a gut strung banjo when the name of Elwood Baines came up. Then as he talked, the nervousness seemed to wear thin and vanish. At the last he was showing all sorts of strength and making signs as if he was the one in control of the conversation. Maybe he had been. Still there was no chance to eliminate him as a potential suspect in the damage done to Elwood Baines.

Buckskin remembered the report of the undertaker. Baines had been castrated *before* he died, accounting for the bleeding in the area. That castration demonstrated a lot of hatred. Why the hatred and who was involved? Two more questions Buckskin had to find answers for, and the quicker the better.

The dead man's lawyer would be next. Only next probably would be tomorrow morning. It was now stone dead and dark. Only a few business firms had lights on and they were closing, except for the saloons and cafes.

He prowled the street just to locate the lawyer's office. He found the shingle hung just outside a street level office half a block down from the newspaper office. The lawyer had lamps burning inside his office. Buckskin tried the knob and found the door unlocked. He knocked, then pushed the door open and walked inside. Now was better than tomorrow.

It was an austere office. Plain wood floor, inexpensive wooden desk, two file boxes in one corner, a picture of a family on the wall. The ceiling and all four walls had been papered. Two lamps threw out their light and revealed a thin man hunched behind the desk. He had an uncontrolled mass of dark hair and his head snapped up when he heard Buckskin come in. The man stood slowly and Buckskin didn't think he would stop. He was at least six-feet six, and wore an all black suit with a black vest and starkly white shirt and dark tie.

"Yes, sir, may I help you?" the thin man said with a voice that sprayed out magnolia blossoms and dripped with honey and rosewater.

"I hope so," Buckskin said walking toward the desk. He held out his hand. "I'm Lee Morgan, in town trying to find out who killed Elwood Baines."

The tall man, with mutton chop sideburns that came nearly to his chin and met his moustache on both sides, ignored the thrust out hand.

"I know why you're here, Mr. Morgan. You must realize that Mr. Baines was my client, so I have the lawyer-client relationship that means I can't say a word about his affairs or his conversations."

"That relationship died when Baines did, Mr. Pickering. We both know that, so enough of the bluffing. If you don't help me, I'll find out what I want to know anyway, and I'll look long and with a certain amount of suspicion at you. If you're not involved in the man's death, what do you have to lose?"

Adler Pickering sat down. Buckskin pegged him at thirty-five or a year older. He had no idea of the quality of the man's training. Here, as in most of the Western states and territories, little formal study was required to be admitted to the practice of law.

Pickering stared at Buckskin a moment, then waved him to the chair that sat near his desk.

"Why not? Everyone in town knows I handled Elwood's affairs. What do you want to know?"

"Any idea who hated him enough to kill him?"

Pickering stared at the ceiling and let out a sigh. "I could make you a list, a long one. Elwood was not subtle in his business dealings or his personal relationships. If he wanted something, he usually took it. Sometimes that was legal and sometimes done with bluff and bravado and threats. It worked. He was the richest man in the county, and I don't mind saying I hated to lose that kind of a client."

"Could you give me a list of names of men who either had threatened to kill him or had reason to?"

"No. That could ruin some good men. A lot of folks around here don't want this dug up. It can only lead to more suffering for the town and the man's family."

"His brother and his widow have both hired me to find the killer."

"Raquel Baines hired you? I find that hard to believe." He shrugged. "All right, it's up to them. What do you want to know besides that list I can't formulate?"

"The names of the stores that Mrs. Baines now owns here in town."

"I can do that. What else?"

"Half the folks in town expect a branch line railroad to be built from Rock Creek up here to Jackson. How big a part in that did Elwood Baines play?"

Pickering threw down his pencil on a pad of paper. "You know about that, too? You work fast, Mr. Morgan. Unfortunately, I know little of that plan. I knew that Mr. Baines had something to do with it. He paraded those trainmen from Chicago around town like they were prize animals on show. He told me there was nothing legal for me to be concerned with yet. When he had some agreements he needed drawn, he'd bring me in on it. Then he died."

"So they were nearing agreement on the line?"

Pickering laughed. "Mr. Morgan. I've seen more than half a dozen deals for a spur line up here. It seems to happen every two years or so. This is only the latest one. The problem is always money. It takes a tremendous amount of cash to start a railroad. Don't plan on selling those land grant sections until long after the line is up, running, and making a profit on its own."

"Then tell me this. Could Baines have been a target for murder because he was involved with another try for a branch rail line into Jackson?"

Pickering sat down and lit a thick brown cigar, blew a mouthful of smoke at the ceiling and tapped the stogie on an ashtray on his desk. "Could have been. Hell, anything is possible. But in this case, Mr. Morgan, I'd say the railroad line couldn't have had much to do with the death."

He leaned forward. "Morgan, you know about the shotgunning on his legs. A dirty, heinous way to shoot a man. Evidently he was on his way to town, shotgunned in the legs and heading for the doctor's office so he wouldn't bleed to death. Shooting a man in the legs that way was either a terrible act of vengeance, or a stupid mistake. I can't figure out either one.

"If the shooter hated the man so much, why would he shoot him and then let him drive toward the doctor's office? Why not hold him there and make him suffer while he died? A lot of questions here I don't know the answers to."

"So the shotgunner was one person, and the six-gun wielded by a second man?" Buckskin asked.

Pickering shook his head. "I didn't say that. I'm just opening up some avenues for you to think about."

"I have. There were two gunmen, maybe others involved in the death."

"Others? How?" Pickering had leaned forward on his desk again.

"Detectives also have a privileged relationship with clients, Mr. Pickering. I'm afraid that's all I can say about that subject."

Pickering stared at Buckskin for an unending thirty seconds, then nodded. "The old bluff and fishing routine. Surprised that you'd even try it on me. I've used it in court a hundred times. But it works only when they don't know it's coming.

"Well, it was interesting talking with you, Mr. Morgan. I still have several legal matters to take care of on the Baines estate. You know by now how it was divided. If there's anything else I can do for you, be sure to give me a visit." Pickering stood and so did Buckskin. The talk was over.

Just as Buckskin got to the door he turned. "Oh, Pickering, I figure you deserve to know a little more. Sometime before he was shotgunned, your former client was poisoned. Thought you'd want to know that." Buckskin caught the surprised expression on the lawyer's face, then the detective swept out the door and walked down the street. Let the legal eagle worry about that one for a while.

Whores.

How had Mrs. Baines put it? She and Elwood had been sleeping in separate bedrooms for the past six years, or was it eight? What did a grown man do when his wife shut him off and he came to town regularly? Whores.

There were only two houses of ill repute in town. He inspected both. The first was off the main street and up a flight of steps. He watched the stairs for ten minutes and saw two range dressed cowhands come down, a kid no more than sixteen, and two drunks.

He moved on to the next home of soiled doves. It was in a neatly painted two-story house half a block off Main Street. This would be the one that Baines would use. Hell, he might even own it. Buckskin walked in and found an ordinary residence's front room. No girls, no men waiting. He looked around the room and saw doilies done in cross stitch: 'Home Sweet Home,' 'Work For The Night Is Coming.'

A woman cleared her throat from a door at the near side of the big room. She looked about forty, wore a dressing robe, had blonde hair piled on top of her head and wore a derringer in a small holster on her right hip. Her face was heavily made up with bright red lips and pink rouge spots on her cheeks.

"Something I can do for you? I'm Gretchen and I run this establishment."

He explained his mission and the woman grinned. "Gonna be strange having that wife of Elwood's running a whorehouse. He owned it, you know. Not that she could work here herself."

"Elwood came here often?"

"Twice a week regular like a railroad man's watch. Now and then he wouldn't come for a month or two. Then about six months ago he stopped showing up. Told me he had something special. Hey, I never question the boss."

"Something special. He ever say what he meant by that?"

"Town woman, I'd guess. Can't figure out who she might be."

"What kind of girl did he want when he came here? Big breasts, good legs, redheads, what?"

"You don't know our Elwood. He wanted the youngest, least experienced girl we had. I used a sixteen-year-old for a while. Elwood couldn't get enough of her."

"So he liked them young. Interesting. Well, I guess I've learned all I can about him here."

"You trying to find out who killed him, I hear."

"Right. You have any ideas along that line?"

The madam shook her head. "Not my line of work. I got me enough trouble trying to keep my six girls happy, not pulling out each other's hair and taking care of the ugly duckling in the batch. Always have one who ain't a beauty, know what I mean? Most men don't mind how good a girl looks long as she takes care of them"

Buckskin watched the woman. She wasn't as old as she looked. Must have worked the trade in her time.

She grinned at him. "What do you think? Can old Gretchen still please a man?"

He laughed. "You can and you damn well know it. But for the record I want you to know that I never pay for love. I'm not a good prospect." He bent and kissed her powdered cheek. "But thanks for the thought, and for the information."

Gretchen beamed. "Hey, you spiced up my whole day. Get out of here and track down the bastard who put that bullet in Elwood. What I hate is that

57

somebody castrated Elwood before they killed him. Get that shitty bastard!"

Buckskin was out the door and back to Main Street before it hit him. Gretchen knew that Elwood had been castrated. How did she know that? Did someone tell her? He ran back hoping he'd found a break in the stone wall.

Gretchen grinned when he opened the door the second time.

"Hey, you back for another session already?" she asked.

This time there were two men in the big living room. She walked over and put her hand through his arm and guided him over to the far door.

"What you said just before I left. How did you know that Elwood had been castrated?"

She laughed and looked back at the other men. "Some of these pokers talk their heads off when they're trying to make it. Especially the ones who have trouble. Somebody told one of the girls, who told me. I'll have to check at breakfast in the morning to find out who told me. She'll remember since it was about the guy who owned this place.

"You staying at the hotel?"

He nodded.

"When I find out I'll send a boy over there with the name of the man who told my girl. Have it sealed up in a white envelope all safe."

Buckskin nodded. "I'll be waiting for it. Just might be a lead I can run down and do some good. So far nothing is making much sense on this one."

He walked back to the hotel. Josh's cafe was closed. He could have used some coffee. He got a pot of coffee and a cup at the hotel dining room and carried it upstairs. The detective wondered if Tilly would be there. Fine either way.

He opened the door to his room and found no lamp burning. No Tilly. He went back over what he had found out today. Met the family of the dead man, three interesting individuals. Met the deceased's lawyer, a man not wholly to be trusted. Made the connection with a father who probably had a pregnant daughter and might be the man who castrated Baines. And he had found out that someone else in town beside him and the undertaker knew about the castration. That could be a big break.

Buckskin locked his door, fired up a coal oil lamp and wrote down notes in the small tablet he carried. The coffee helped him get it all down. He concentrated on the items he didn't want to forget. He needed a good solid lead on this one, needed a lead bad.

Maybe tomorrow.

# Chapter Five

The next morning when Buckskin went down to the desk, there were two messages in his box. One sealed and the other from Tilly which came to the point quickly.

"Tonight for damn sure. Ten o'clock your room. I'll be there. Don't be late. Tilly."

The other note was longer and came from Raquel Baines. The widow's note read: "I may have misjudged you, Mr. Morgan. I have some letters from Chicago that my husband was interested in getting the day he was killed. Please come and look at them and help me decide what to do about them. Can I expect you this morning about ten?"

Buckskin considered the matter as he had a quick breakfast. The Chicago letters. Yes, they could be highly important. No sense waiting until ten, he'd go

60

out right after breakfast. He reconsidered. The lady probably slept late. He'd get there at nine-thirty.

Before he had to leave, Buckskin looked over the handwritten list of properties and businesses that Elwood Baines owned in Jackson. Twelve of them, nearly half the stores in town, including the general store, the livery, the stage, one of the saloons and the bawdy house. All the essential elements of a roaring, growing Western town. Baines must have planned ahead.

Buckskin checked with the general store manager, a gent named Only Kerrigan. He was a bright-eyed redhead and greeted the detective with a hearty handshake.

"Been wanting to meet you, Mr. Morgan. Understand you're going to nail the hide of Mr. Baines' killer to the county courthouse door. I'll volunteer to help skin the bastard when you catch him."

Buckskin grinned. "Don't sharpen up your skinning knives yet. I'm just getting started. Wondered how you could help me."

"Damn, any way that I can."

Two women customers came in and a slight, pretty woman in a bright blue dress came through a curtain to the back room and hurried to wait on the women customers.

"I hear that Baines was something of a slave driver. You worked for him. How did he treat you?"

"First class all the way. He gave me the job of running the store and said all I had to do was satisfy the needs of the people of Jackson and make a profit. So far my wife Nel and I have been doing just that. Don't know what to expect now with Mrs. Baines in the driver's seat. She might even want to sell out, and the Lord knows I couldn't afford to buy this big place."

"Wouldn't worry about that, at least for a time. She's probably snowed under a ten foot drift with everything she has to think about right now."

"Met her a couple of times. Seems like a right nice lady. Of course, sometimes when a person suddenly gets power in her hands she might not know what to do with it, how to use it proper."

"Maybe the family lawyer will help her," Buckskin said.

Only Kerrigan laughed and shook his head. "I sure hope to hell not. Pickering would not be my choice for the ideal lawyer. He's pulled some pretty questionable deals here in town."

Buckskin lifted his brows. "He has? Like what?"

"Oh, nothing he could be put in jail for, just a little bit of sham and shadows here and there, a promise forgotten, a deal made with a handshake that evaporated when the lawsuit came down. Nothing major."

"Thinking of bad actors in town, you have any candidates for the man who killed your boss?"

Only furrowed his brow, then closed his eyes and massaged his face with one hand. When he looked up at Buckskin he shook his head. "Can't give you a suspect, if that's what you're asking. Know lots of folks who didn't like Mr. Baines, but not any who would plot to kill him."

Buckskin held out his hand. "Been good talking with you, Kerrigan. I might want some more background on your ex-boss one of these days. Try to remember anyone in town who might have been mad enough at Baines to do him in. I'd appre~..~ it."

Buckskin walked outside and stood in front of the store a moment. It was on the corner and one of the biggest retail spots in town. He turned and went to the cross street after a team of six passed, when a woman came along the side of the general store and waved to him. She motioned for him to come down the side of the store.

He looked again and recognized the slight, pretty woman from the general store in the bright blue dress. He walked that way and she led him to the back of the store and stood behind a stack of lumber.

"Mr. Morgan, I heard what you and Only were talking about. I . . . I don't know if I should tell you this, but I at last decided that I should. You were asking about somebody furious enough with Mr. Baines to kill him. I know one man who was.

"It was about six months ago and I was in the store alone. Only had gone to the bank. Mr. Baines came in and we talked. He had always been kind to me. This time he asked to see Only and I told him he'd just left for the Bank and would be gone for a half hour.

"He nodded, then asked me to show him the back stock. As soon as we were through the curtain into the rear of the store, he grabbed me and kissed me. He pushed me against the wall and tore at my blouse." She looked away. "I've never told anyone this before, Mr. Morgan. It's embarrassing, but I decided you should know. Sometimes Mr. Baines was not nice at all."

"Did he hurt you?"

"No, he didn't get that far. He did have my blouse and chemise ripped off so I was . . . I was bare to the waist. His hands were all over me and he even kissed my breasts. Just then Only came in. He'd forgotten part of his deposit and he flew at Mr. Baines and punched him three or four times before he knocked him down.

"Mr. Baines pulled out a derringer and fired into the ceiling and Only backed off. Mr. Baines said if either one of us ever told anyone about this, he'd charge us with embezzling money from the store and send us both to prison."

Buckskin touched the woman's shoulder. "I appreciate your telling me this. I know it was hard for you. I won't let your husband know you told me. Now for the important question. Do you think Only is still furious enough that he could have killed Elwood Baines?"

The slight woman looked up, fear and worry shrouding her pretty face. Slowly she shook her head. "I . . . I just can't say one way or the other. He was livid for days. He wouldn't let me talk about it, he wouldn't touch me for a month. Slowly he got over it. I've never seen him so angry before.

"When he knocked Mr. Baines down, he was in such a rage I think he might have killed him. Now, to plan it, to think it through and then do it. . . . I don't know if he could do that or not."

She rubbed tears away from her eyes. "You live with a man for years and then this happens and you never realized that he loved you so much."

She turned away and went into the store.

Buckskin stood there after she had gone. He had his first suspect in the killing. From what his wife said, Only Kerrigan might very well have been one of the men to have at least tried to kill the rancher. But if he did, which of the four methods did he use?

Buckskin checked his pocket watch. Time to get a horse and head out to the Baines ranch. Second time in two days. It would be a quicker trip today. He was more than curious about the Chicago letters. His great hope was that they would name some names and give him a good solid suspect in the murder. Or did he need four suspects?

The more he considered it, the more confident he was that the four assaults on Elwood Baines had been done by four separate persons. Which brought him back to the point about which of the attacks killed him.

This time when he rode into the ranch yard at the Box B spread, a hand took his horse and Mrs. Baines was waiting for him near the kitchen door.

"Glad you could come, Mr. Morgan. I have something I hope you can explain. Two letters came from Chicago. Midge said her father told her he had to go to town to get them that last night. They came regular mail, so the postmistress put them with our other mail. I can't fathom them."

They went into the house, through to a den and to a large desk with two handwritten letters on top.

"Take a look," she said.

Buckskin picked up the first one page letter and read it. It didn't make a lot of sense to him. It was about the branch line they were calling the Rock Springs and Jackson Railroad. He read the letter again and concentrated on the last paragraph.

"Therefore, Mr. Baines, I'm counting on you to provide the enabling power on your end to make this

## Kit Dalton

venture work. It's not totally financed yet, but should be within two weeks at the latest. Then we'll need rights of way into Jackson and spur lines from there out to the timber. We're counting on you to get those rights of way and all other permissions we'll need."

Buckskin looked up with the picture a little bit clearer. "Does Jackson have a city council or a mayor?"

"Did have a mayor," Mrs. Baines said. "Elwood bought a house in town just so he could run for mayor. He got elected the last two terms."

"So he could grease the skids as needed to get the railroad into town?"

"I suppose so. But what was he going to get out of it? Elwood seldom went to this much trouble without a good sized stake in the outcome."

Buckskin looked over the second letter but it said about the same thing. Nothing at all about any shares of stock or holdings that Elwood Baines would receive for his services.

"There could be some verbal agreements."

Mrs. Baines shook her head. "Not by Elwood. He had to have everything down in black and white, two copies and signed by all parties concerned and with two witnesses."

"I understand there are some people in town opposed to the railroad."

"Yes. A kind of vocal minority. Nobody I can think of who has any power or influence. If the rails get here most folks will applaud them."

Buckskin read the letters again, then handed them to Mrs. Baines. "I can't see anything unusual or tremendously important here. Everyone knew that your husband was working to get the rail line in here. This

66

just says the same thing." He stood from where he had been and nodded to the woman.

"I thank you for the information. Who knows, it might add up to something down the line somewhere. I have some other business in town, so I better ride back that way."

"Oh, I thought you might have a cup of coffee and a roll."

"Thanks, but I better be on my way."

Five minutes later he had mounted his horse and ridden down the lane that led along the mighty Snake River and toward town. He had just rounded a bend in the river when he saw a rider ahead stopped near the side of the trail.

As he came closer he saw the person on the horse was a woman, a young girl. A moment later he knew it was Midge. Buckskin pulled alongside her and stopped.

She wore a tight blouse, cut down men's jeans, and rode astride.

"Well, you certainly talked with Mother long enough. I didn't think you would ever come out. Some big important meeting?"

"No, we just talked about the letters from Chicago. They must not have been as important as your father thought."

"I decided that when they came." She motioned to him. "Come over here, I want to show you something." She rode into the woods along the bank of the Snake. Midge swung down from her mount and ground tied her, then motioned again.

"Come over here, we can't ride where I want to take you. You'll be fascinated by the sight, I'd just bet."

"What in the world are you talking about?"

"A brand new beaver colony. They don't have to build a dam, plenty of water along the river bank. They've been working so hard on getting their house all fixed." She grinned. "Come on and take a look. Up the bank about twenty yards."

He swung down and followed her. The cut down jeans fit her so tightly they outlined her round little bottom. She stopped and pointed ahead a dozen feet. Two beavers worked on the house that had an underwater entrance and an above water living space.

"Figured the beaver were all trapped out along here."

"They were, but that was back in the forties. Now they have multiplied all over the place."

She sat down on a grassy spot of the bank and watched the beavers. He sat down three feet away, watching them.

"You know you shouldn't be here alone with me, don't you, Midge?"

She turned and looked at him, serious for a moment, then she smiled. "Yes, of course. That's mostly why I lured you in here. Don't worry, I'm not an innocent little virgin." She unbuttoned the top four fasteners on her blouse and he could see the swell of her bare breasts. She had on nothing under the blouse.

"I wouldn't scare you away now, Buckskin, would I?" She undid the rest of the buttons and held the front of the blouse out to show him her breasts. They were still high on her chest, pointing slightly upward and still forming, not yet entirely rounded but more like peaks.

She moved toward him on her hands and knees, her breasts swinging and swaying as she moved. They fascinated Buckskin.

"Don't think you're ruining me or anything like that. I've . . . I've been making love since I was thirteen. I love it, I really get charged up." She slid beside him and reached over and kissed his lips. Then again. Her tongue worked into his mouth and she found his hand and brought it to her young breasts.

"Damn, but you are a tease, Midge. I'm not like the young boys your age. They would have shot their load in their pants by now. You get me worked up, I'll want more."

"You'll get all you want, Buckskin. I've never messed around with boys my age. I like older men."

Her fingers found his growing erection through his pants and she rubbed it until Buckskin moaned softly. He caught her and kissed her hungrily, pushing her down on the grass on her back and lying on top of her.

"Yes, yes, yes, Buckskin. I want you inside me. Let me get these damn pants off. Skirts are so much easier. Help me, damn you."

He pulled her boots off, then the tight jeans and she had nothing on under them either. Midge was sleek and young, so unspoiled and unmarked that she made him catch his breath. She was sturdier than her mother, more rounded, with a flat little belly and a swatch of brown crotch hair.

He stroked it and she whimpered. He went to her breasts, licking them, then kissing them until she began to squirm under him. He bit her nipples until they hardened and she pushed her legs apart and ripped open the buttons on his fly.

"Right now, Buckskin. Do me right now before I die. I want you inside me hard and fast and faster. Do me right now, Buckskin, before I die. I want you to fuck me so bad I'll beg you."

He lifted his hips and she guided him. A moment later she wailed as he powered into her slippery sheath. She took all of him and pushed upward for more. Then she began to gyrate her hips and a moment later he felt his own passion growing. She hadn't made a sign that she was close.

Buckskin could wait no longer. He drove into her again and again, pushing her upward on the soft grass, staining his knees with green and not caring.

When he recovered he looked down at her and saw tears seeping from her eyes.

"You didn't make it," he said.

"Never do, never have. I always keep hoping that maybe this time it will work."

"Then why do you keep trying? Let it settle down. Let your body finish growing up. You have lots of time."

"No, I want to get fucked and climax like the other women do. I've heard them talk. They go wild, they say. Absolutely wild and will do anything to get it again. I don't feel that. Just the first push is fantastic, but it doesn't get any better."

He helped her dress.

"Don't rush growing up. You're a kid such a short time and then come the tough realities of life. Remember that into every happiness a little life must fall. Just try to take it easy."

"Again. Maybe this time with my clothes on and I can—" He put his fingers over her lips.

"No. You'll be missed at the ranch, and I have to get into town. It isn't right, a man my age and a girl your age."

"Age has nothing to do with it."

"Don't remind me. Now I'm getting out of here before your brother and the hands lynch me." He grinned. "Midge, you were fantastic. You got me so hot so fast and wanting you so much that I just rode right over the fact that you're not really old enough. You were terrific. In another five years. . . . wow."

She pulled on her boots and scowled. "You're saying that just because you got to fuck me."

"True, but what I said is true also. You'll be a beautiful, sexy woman. Just give yourself three years, at least."

She clung to him as they said goodbye just inside the tree line. Then she rode along the trees and would go well north of the ranch before she came out.

Buckskin surged onto the town trail and pounded along hard for half a mile, then eased off and walked his mount the rest of the way into town. Midge was a bed full already. Damn, what she would be in three or four years would be something.

Back at the hotel, he checked his room box. No messages. Upstairs he found Tilly cleaning a room next to his. He grinned at her and she scowled at him.

"I work here, remember? Some of us have to work for a living." She motioned into his room and hurried in after him when she saw no one watching her. She closed the door and kissed him.

"Hey, I can smell another woman on you."

"Just my new bay rum and rose water aftershave lotion," Buckskin said. "Anything more on our little bitch in heat?"

"Oh yes. She left on the morning stage for Rock Springs and from there to Omaha. Her best friend in the whole world found out for sure and she told us. Little miss hot pussy got diddled once too often at the wrong time of the month. She's three months pregnant and already showing."

"I talked with her father."

"But you didn't ask him if somebody popped a bean in his daughter's little hole, did you?"

Buckskin grinned. He'd never heard that way of saying someone got pregnant. "Not exactly, in fact, not at all. I just wanted to sound him out. He acted a little strange. If he had something to do with a killing, he covered it up well. I'll have to go see him again."

"But not tonight. I get off at ten and we have a date in your bed."

"I can't tonight. A late meeting and an early up in the morning."

She frowned, dropped her small fists to her waist and confronted him head on. "Don't just shut me off this way, Buckskin."

"I'm not. I just can't be with you tonight."

"You're seeing another woman."

"Sure, I've got the hots for Gretchen over at the bawdy house."

Tilly giggled. "I can just see you trying to find it among all those rolls of fat."

"Don't be sassy. Wait until you're forty."

"Damn, no! I don't ever want to live that long. I'll be old and dried up like a prune and almost dead." She frowned and looked up. "Oh, sorry. You're closer to forty than I am and you're far from dried up and dead."

"Thanks. Now, I need to do some more calling on store owners. Somewhere there's a man or two who knows exactly what happened the night Baines died. I have to dig them out and get them to tell me and the sheriff."

He worked at it all afternoon until he had called on every store and business that Elwood Baines had owned. Nowhere did he find any anger or hatred. Certainly nothing that would stir up enough fury to lead to murder. Twice he had walked past the doctor's office.

He stopped and read the shingle. "Dr. Newton Ralston, General Medicine, Surgery."

Maybe he needed another medical opinion on the blue lips meant poison theory of the undertaker. He could live with the decision one way or the other, but the poisoning did make the case more interesting.

Buckskin pushed the door open and walked into the empty waiting room.

# Chapter Six

A face appeared in an opening in the near wall of the doctor's office. It was round with a full beard and wire rim spectacles. The face smiled.

"Well, the detective. About time you came to see me. Hear you talked to the undertaker first. That ruffled my feathers a little but not a lot. I'll be right out."

The face vanished from the foot square window and a door opened along the wall. The man who came out was small, thin, compact, vigorous and wore a stained white shirt, no tie and brown town pants. He held out his hand.

They shook and both sat down on the hard wooden benches in the waiting room.

"I'm Doc Ralston, Newt to most everyone in town. Hell, I birthed half the folks here, it seems. Don't guess, I'll be glad to tell you how old I am. Sixty-six come next month, and no I don't plan on quitting and sitting in a rocking chair somewhere bitching about everything.

"I'm a nut about work. I get in twelve to fifteen hours most days and maybe only half that on Sundays. I'm going to go right on practicing until I'm ninety-two. Then I'll pay some whippersnapper with a medical degree to take my place here, roll me over in a ditch somewhere and let me die."

Doc Ralston grinned. "I give that little harangue when I meet a new person or a new patient, so they damn well know who and what they're dealing with. You must be Buckskin Morgan. Why aren't you wearing buckskin clothes?"

Buckskin grinned. "Because they're hot as hell in the summertime, get stiff in the winter. I once got caught in a snowdrift in my buckskins. Couldn't move. My buckskins froze stiff and when they found me they turned up my toes and hooked two dogs on me and towed me out just like a dog sled. I didn't unfreeze for three days and they sledded me halfway down the mountain."

Doc Ralston chuckled. "Yeah, I like that. A man with some imagination and a gift of gab, to coin a phrase. What's your diagnosis on this Elwood Baines killing?"

"You're the doctor, you tell me what happened to him."

"Most you already know. A shotgun round at medium range but aimed low, mangled his legs. Surprised he made it into a buggy. Some time after that somebody caught him in his weakened state and performed a rather primitive bilateral orchiectomy. Sliced both his balls off, but you knew that.

"He survived that and the wound had almost stopped bleeding when someone put a large caliber slug through the back of his head. There was a three-inch powder burn on his skin and hair, so the muzzle was no more than six inches away from his head when the round was fired."

"Is that it, nothing else?"

"What do you mean, detective man?"

"Blue lips."

Doc Ralston chuckled again. Buckskin had taken to the old sawbones at once. He was sharp and clever.

"You know about that. Thought that was my little secret with the digger man. Yep, near as I could tell Elwood Baines had been poisoned and was close to death from the strychnine. Not a chance he could have lived through a dose like that. The slug in the head just quickened matters."

"Strychnine. Is that hard to find around Jackson?"

"About as hard as going to the store and buying rat poison. Most of it takes about half an hour to work. Not pretty and painful as all hell."

"A half hour. Where was the body found?"

"Outside of town." The doctor nodded. "Oh, yes, I see. Did he come straight from his ranch. Not really. He was found on the far side of town from his place. He could have met someone in town and been driven out there. He could have been shotgunned in town, poisoned here as well, and then taken the forty-five slug."

'Which means we have a whole town full of suspects." Buckskin scowled. "You're not one hell of a lot of help, Doc."

"Didn't claim to be. You're the detective."

Buckskin grinned. "Yeah, I hope. Anything else that might give me a clue as to what happened to Baines?"

"Afraid not. Sheriff's got his valuables. But then if a killer went to this much trouble, he'd take anything from the body that would incriminate him. Guess you're on your own."

"Doc, I know you can't tell me, but have you seen many pregnant unmarried young girls lately?"

The old medic looked at Buckskin sharply, then nodded. "The castration. You figure Baines was screwing around and some angry father took out his rusty knife and fixed Baines so he wouldn't get another young girl in trouble."

"Could have happened that way."

"Yeah, probably did." He rubbed his jaw. "But the man with the knife didn't kill Baines. He made sure that the bleeding stopped. He used some wooden clothespins to keep the ragged edges of the scrotum together so he wouldn't bleed to death. That tells me that he wasn't trying to kill the man, just make him suffer for the rest of his life. He wanted Baines to live."

"So who in town fits that description, the father of a young girl in a family way?"

"Mr. Morgan, I'd like to tell you, I truly would. The trouble is most women in this town don't come to see me until they're in their seventh or eighth month of pregnancy. The girl's mother would know, and her father. Maybe her best friend. The stage company is a better bet for finding your girl than I am. Look to see who is getting out of town quickly."

"All right, but have you heard of any rumors? Any young girl doing a lot of bedding down around town, somebody taking on all comers just for the fun of it?"

"Sure, I know of two or three. Two of them have venereal disease and I've warned them. Neither of them is pregnant. The other one, I'm not sure about. She's never come to see me about her privates."

"I thought in a small town everyone knew everyone else's business," Buckskin said.

"Mostly. The other young girls would be the ones to talk to."

"I did. I have a candidate."

The old medic's eyes brightened and he looked at Buckskin with the grin of a gossip. "Now just who have the young girls been whispering about?"

"You know Irene Channing?"

The doctor was quiet for a minute. He shook his head. "The preacher's girl. Hell yes, I know her. Birthed her. Chicken pox, whooping cough and measles twice. Damn right I know her and the whole family. Irene is a quiet girl, always respectful of her elders. Does exactly what her father says."

"Does the preacher hold a tight rein on the girl?"

"Of course. I hear she's not the brightest girl in school but good around the house."

Buckskin nodded. "Makes you wonder then, doesn't it. Just why do you suppose the preacher sent his daughter off to Omaha this morning to go on to more schooling?"

"He did?"

"That's my best information."

The doctor stretched his feet out and shook his head. "Ever had a high spirited horse that you held to a gentle walk maybe for days. Then there came a point where he just couldn't stand it anymore and he threw the bit and took off across country at the fastest gallop he could manage?"

"Seen it happen once. You're saying the preacher might have held the girl down so long that she rebelled, did exactly what he told her not to and soon wound up pregnant?"

"Been known to happen." He tapped his foot on the floor. "Especially seeing that his Irene never really graduated from the tenth grade. They kind of eased her out to get rid of her. Oh, I know about that, I'm on the school board."

Buckskin stood and paced the waiting room. "Even if Channing did the cutting, it would be almost impossible to prove in court if he denied it. A lot of fathers would vote not to convict him if it went that far.

"On the other hand, a confrontation and a threat might get me some facts about where the buggy was when he cut the man, who he saw, what he saw." Buckskin shook the surprised medic's hand.

"Thanks, Doc. You may have helped me fill in one of the puzzle pieces. But I need a lot more. Getting back to the poison, I still wonder who slipped Baines the rat poison."

"I've heard that good strong coffee masks the taste pretty well," Doc Ralston said. "Never tried it myself."

"Somebody sure did. Where would a man heading for the postmaster's place stop and get coffee?"

Doc Ralston frowned. "At his brother's cafe?"

"Maybe. But then why hire me to find out who killed him? I don't read Josh that way. Baines didn't get the poison in his brother's cafe."

"He could have had coffee at home before he left," Doc said.

"Three miles in a buggy is about twenty minutes. Possible. But why would his wife want to kill the goose laying the golden eggs every few days?"

Doc Ralston nodded. "I agree. I know the woman. She isn't the type to kill her own husband. They don't get on the best, but she just isn't up to murder."

"Probably, but poison is a woman's favorite murder weapon."

"You know that, most men do, so maybe a man used poison to throw you off the track."

Buckskin groaned. "Doc, I came here to make things clearer for me, not so you could murk up the waters even more."

"Sorry. I'm a reader of novels where somebody tries to solve a murder. Some good English ones out that I'm trying to find."

Buckskin stood and twirled his hat. "You get any more wild ideas about who killed Baines, Doc, you let me know. I'm at the hotel. Right now I think it's time that I pay another call on my pastor, the Rev. Dwight Channing."

They said goodbye and Buckskin went out into the noontime sunshine. He had a quick lunch at Josh's Grand Teton Cafe and then strolled down the street to the parsonage beside the church with the white painted steeple.

The pastor was in. "Mr. Morgan. It seems we talked only last night."

"That's true, Reverend Channing. But I've learned a few things since then that we need to go over. Maybe we should take a walk and have some privacy."

The pastor frowned, shrugged and they went back outside and walked toward the edge of town a block away.

"I hear your daughter, Irene, is going to Omaha to continue her schooling."

The preacher frowned, then lifted a brow and nodded. "That's right. A good school there where she can study to be a nurse and stay with her aunt."

"Sounds convenient. I also understand that Irene was a rather poor student and that she isn't qualified to enter a nursing school."

The preacher stopped and scowled at Morgan. "That's . . . that's none of your business."

"Oh, but I'm afraid that it is, Mr. Channing. You see, I know that Irene is pregnant."

The look of fury that jolted over Channing's face was awesome in its stark hatred. The man struggled to control himself for a few seconds. His first words blurted out but he stopped them almost at once. "That's not true, she's—"

Channing turned and walked ahead slowly. He shook his head in silent anger and denial. At last he looked up. "How did you know?"

"I wasn't positive until just now, but most girls who get pushed out of the tenth grade don't go into a tough academic program like nursing. Then the rumors going around town pegged her as being in a family way."

"So now you know. How does this concern you?"

"She doesn't. You do. Only three of us in town know that Elwood Baines was castrated before he died. Now I'm sure that you're the angry father who did it. You did, didn't you?"

They walked half a block before the preacher could say a word. He had tried several times but nothing came out. At last he stopped and touched Morgan's shoulder.

"I didn't plan on doing it. I just wanted to vent my rage at him. Show how he had ruined a young girl and demand that he support her with a hundred dollars a month and take responsibility for raising the child.

"He laughed at me, but I could see he was in pain. I tore off a lap robe he had over his legs. I've never seen human legs so shot up, so bloody. I was surprised the man had any blood left.

"He lashed out at me with all the vile and filthy words he knew, then he passed out. It was a spur of the moment thing. I pulled out my old pocket knife and tore open his trousers and cut his balls off. Then I tried to keep him from bleeding to death and got his buggy going toward the center of town. It was dark but I figured someone would find him and get him to Doc Ralston."

Buckskin nodded and pointed a finger at him. "What you just told me could send you away to state prison for ten years. You must know that. You have one chance. Tell me exactly where the buggy was when you found it. Tell me everything that Baines told you. I want to know who hit him with the shotgun round. Tell me everything both of you said."

Channing nodded and went over it slowly.

"I first saw the buggy as it came toward town past the church. It was going slow. I ran after it, caught it and saw that Baines was in it and either drunk or sick. I figured it was the best time to confront him.

"I stopped the buggy at Third and Almont, that's the first block north of Main. We were about three blocks from the center of town. He was conscious so I had it out with him. Irene told me that he had been using her for two months, sometimes twice a day.

"He laughed at me. I tried to hit him but he lifted a .45 derringer and pointed it at me. I screamed at him and told him I'd tell everyone in town what he'd done. He tried to shoot me but the round missed. Then he passed out.

"I figured that was my chance. I ripped open his pants and saw his shot up legs and I went ahead and cut him like I told you."

"Did you see anyone else around the buggy during this time?"

"No sir."

"Did anyone come and talk to you just before, during or just after your talk with Baines?"

"No, not a soul."

Buckskin smiled at the man. "Look, I know you're upset. You were frightened half to death that night and you had good reason to be. But try to think back slowly, clearly. Did you see anyone at all in the houses or on the street, under the splash of light from a building, anyone riding past or coming toward you?"

"I saw the buggy. I recognized it as belonging to Baines. I've seen it often enough near our home. Irene and her mother told me that night that she was pregnant and who had done it, so I was furious. I went looking for Baines.

"Then, even before I got downtown, I saw him driving in. But he wasn't coming to my place. Evidently he was angling toward Doc Ralston's office. I yelled at him, then chased the buggy. He slowed.

"Oh, yes, a team hauling a farm wagon with some kind of grain in it was crossing the street and he had to stop for it. That's how I caught him. I jumped inside the buggy and put my knife against his side and he glared at me."

"What did Baines say?"

"He screamed, said he was hurt bad, going to see the doctor. I said he didn't look hurt to me. He let go of the reins and the rig stopped. I accused him of getting Irene pregnant and he said that was between her and him. She was big enough to know what she was doing.

"I pushed the point of my knife through his shirt and brought blood from his side. He drew his Derringer and tried to shoot me, but he was in a bad way, weaving and falling against the side of the rig. He shot, missed and I took the weapon away from him.

"Then he passed out and I cut him. When I left the buggy the horse just stood there. I remembered he was going to see Doc Ralston, so I whacked the roan and it walked on down the street. I didn't see anybody on the street or going into any of the houses along there."

"Did you follow the buggy?"

"No, I watched it for half a block, then I turned and ran for home. I threw away my knife. I never wanted to see it again, especially not with the rapist's blood on it."

"Did you keep the derringer?" Buckskin asked.

"Oh no. When I cut him I put the weapon down on the seat and spread his legs wide."

"What time did you get home?"

"It was dark by then, full dark when I left the buggy. Must have been seven, seven-thirty."

"Who was driving the farm wagon?"

"Oh, that was Old Caleb. Only name I know him by. Has a small farm north of town aways."

"Good. Do you remember seeing anyone else? Close your eyes and go over the time you were chasing the buggy."

"Oh, back that far. Well, there was a woman turning into her house. She comes to church sometimes. She's older and never wears her hair in a bun. My wife knows her name."

"That's fine, I'm more interested in any men you saw."

"No sir, that was it, just Old Caleb."

"Fine, Mr. Channing. I can't promise you won't be charged for what you diu. I'll see what else happens. I'd guess about now you have a few sins of your own to worry about."

Buckskin turned and walked away, leaving the preacher standing on the empty street with his head down and shoulders slumped.

Buckskin knew a lot more about the death of Elwood Baines, but not the most important parts: who poisoned him, who shotgunned him, and who killed him with the slug in the back of the head?

The derringer.

The police report listed no weapon as being found at the scene. The preacher didn't take the derringer.

Where had it gone? What happened to it and was it the murder gun?

A large caliber derringer at close range produces deadly results as well as a circular powder burn. Yes, it could have been Baines' own derringer that killed him. But who pulled the trigger?

At Main Street, he saw the dust coming and watched with wonder as the stage coach pulled into town. Out between towns the coaches struggle up hills, roll across the level stretches leisurely, but when they came into town the whip cracked and the horses galloped and the rig raced down Main Street with a cloud of dust and snorting horses as a few town boys tried to run alongside. The rig screeched to a halt at the stage depot with the binders tightening down on the wooden wheels, producing another storm of dust.

Buckskin walked that way as the driver jumped down, opened the door and let the passengers out. Someone on the roof began tossing down bags, satchels and boxes. The driver went to the back and opened the boot, taking out more baggage and a few boxes of rush freight.

When the local passengers had all left for home, three newly arrived men in dark suits stood on the boardwalk near the depot looking around. One checked the time on his pocket watch. A second took off his town hat, turned it in his hands once and put it back on. The third pointed down the street and said something and the three moved in that direction. They came toward Buckskin.

They walked three abreast down the planking and people moved aside for them. They had gone a short way when another man wearing a black suit and vest hurried up to them. He shook hands all around and it was only when he turned and led the three men toward a nearby office that Buckskin identified the local man.

The greeter was Adler Pickering, lawyer and right hand man to Elwood Baines. Slowly the gears meshed in Buckskin's brain. Three men in dark suits had come to Jackson before. They must be the three railroad men who had come to town when Baines squired them around.

Now the lawyer Pickering seemed to be filling in for his dead client. Was that enough of a motive for murder? But Baines had no money stake in the railroad that anybody knew about. Or did he? Could Pickering pick up where his boss had left off and collect the bounty? There had to be a money or land stake here, and it looked like lawyer Adler Pickering had swung right into step to pick up the spoils, if he could deliver on the promises.

Buckskin walked toward the Pickering office. Time to find out right now where the motives lay. He would be an uninvited guest at the conference in the lawyer's office. He reached for the doorknob and grinned, wondering who would be more surprised, the three railroad men or lawyer Pickering.

# Chapter Seven

Buckskin didn't bother to knock on the lawyer's door. He thrust it open and stepped inside. Four surprised faces turned toward him.

"Gentlemen. My name is Lee Morgan and I'm in town investigating a murder of your former partner here, Elwood Baines."

One of the men stood, his face sober. "We were informed of his death and we offer our sympathy. We know his passing is a great loss to the community."

"Mr. Morgan, you weren't invited to this meeting," lawyer Pickering said. "I'll have to ask you to leave."

"Afraid that's out of the question before I get some answers. I assume that you three gents are from Chicago and have been here before and recently wrote Mr. Baines some letters."

The tall man who stood nodded. "Indeed we are. Mr. Baines was a business associate of ours."

"His widow showed me the letters you wrote to Baines. There was no mention of any consideration for his services. Just what was he to be paid or to gain from your association?"

"None of your damned business, Morgan," Pickering shot back.

The Chicago man smiled. "My name is Dunwoody. I'm chairman of the board of directors of the Rock Creek and Jackson Railroad. I'll be happy to help your murder investigation in any way that I can. Yes, we did have a financial arrangement with Mr. Baines. How much money was involved is proprietary information and I see that it in no way could have any bearing on the investigation of his death."

"Oh, but it does. He was murdered. The potential income from such a venture could be the motive for murder."

The man pondered that a moment. He was well groomed, dressed in an expensive suit and had a fancy knotted tie over his white shirt. He nodded.

"I think we can say that the monetary consideration in land and cash would have been considerable for Mr. Baines. Of course, that contract is now null and void. I am not only the chairman of the board, I'm an attorney as well, Mr. Morgan. Now, does that satisfy your questions?"

"Not quite, Mr. Dunwoody. I assume that Pickering here is taking over the task of smoothing the way for the rail lines into the county and the city?"

"I can't respond to that, Mr. Morgan."

"Proprietary, I know. Without a substantial investment on Mr. Pickering's part, would his return on his labors for you be as great as it would have been for Mr. Baines?"

"Sorry, same answer. Now, It would seem you've run out of questions. This is a closed meeting and we do not have a great deal of time. It would seem prudent for you to take your leave."

"I've never been accused of being prudent before, Mr. Dunwoody. Let me put it this way. If the three of you, or Pickering, had any hand in the death of Elwood Baines, I'll hunt you down and hound you until I find you an extract an extreme measure of justice for the untimely death of Jackson's leading citizen. Do I make myself as clear as a Wyoming morning?"

"You do, Mr. Morgan. Good day."

Buckskin stood there a moment, his hand quivering over his .45, then he grinned, turned and walked out of the office.

So there was a payoff for Baines in his work for the rail line here. What would it have been? Most probably the payment would have been made in land. If the rails got to Jackson, the line would have been land poor. Fifty, maybe sixty or eighty sections of land along the right of way that would be granted by the government could have been Baines' payoff. They would have enough raw land to be generous. Such land grants would have been a legacy of wealth for the Baines family down through the years.

Would have been.

So where did that leave the investigation? The railroad work may have been a motive in the killing. Fine, but a motive for whom? Pickering? Too obvious, too easy to connect. Then who?

Buckskin headed for the hotel. He checked his box and found two notes, both sealed in envelopes. He opened one and read it as he went upstairs. It was from Tilly:

"Tonight for sure. I'm working today. I might see you around the homestead here. If not, then in your room at ten o'clock? I keep hoping."

The second note was in a more genteel hand, carefully crafted in ink on slightly scented paper.

"Mr. Morgan. I need to talk to you again and see how you're progressing on the investigation. I'm at our town house, a block down from the bank up the hill. A three-story house painted white with light blue trim. You can't miss it. I'd like to see you between two and four this afternoon. I hope to see you then." It was signed by Raquel Baines. Interesting.

Buckskin wondered what she wanted. He should ask her for some up front money, expenses. Yes, he'd do that. It wouldn't hurt to get paid by two people. She could afford it.

Between two and four. Easy. It was only a little after two right then and Buckskin realized he hadn't eaten. Had to keep up his strength. He went into his room and washed his hands and face in the porcelain bowl provided and dried off. Then he combed his hair and set his hat on just right.

He was about to head for the door when someone knocked. He opened it from the wall side as always only to see Tilly burst into the room, grinning and swinging the door shut.

"I found you here. Now that's a change." She went to him and kissed him hard, pushing her body firmly against him.

"I know we don't have time right now, but give me a little bit of a petting preview. Chew on my titties."

She pulled open her blouse and there they were.

"I've got to go in a minute," Buckskin said. "Don't get worked up and follow me naked down the hall."

She grinned. "What a delicious idea. I could be naked and holding onto your leg as you dragged me along the hallway."

He bent and kissed her orbs, then teased her nipples and at last kissed them and nibbled on her red nipples until they sprang into full life and throbbed under his tongue.

He pulled away. "I really have to leave."

"I could suck you off real quick. Want me to?"

"You never get enough sex, do you, Tilly? We just don't have time now. Soon, I promise you soon. Hell, I want to get into your bloomers and part those white thighs as much as you want me to. Give me another day or two and I should have this murder all wrapped up. Then we'll do something special."

"Promise?"

"Promise." He buttoned her blouse and paddled her round little bottom on the way to the door.

"Oh, yes. Next time spank me, will you? Makes me all hot and twittering and wild."

"Next time."

She cracked the door open, looked out to check the hall, then hurried out and closed the door behind her.

Buckskin grinned and made sure he was presentable in the crotch area of his body before he went out the door himself. He needed a good midday dinner and then he'd go see Mrs. Baines. He wondered what was on her mind this time.

He checked in with Josh Baines, told him he was making some progress but not in the important areas, had dinner and walked down the street toward the big house where Mrs. Baines evidently now spent some of her time.

He found it as described and rang a twist bell that sounded inside. Almost at once a young woman answered the door.

"Yes sir?"

"Lee Morgan to see Mrs. Baines. I'm expected."

"Lottie, bring Mr. Baines into the parlor, please," a woman's voice said from the other room.

A minute later, Buckskin stood looking down at Raquel Baines, who sat on a couch. She wore a flowered dress that showed a generous amount of bare chest and cinched in tightly at her waist. No longer did she have the starved waif look he had seen so strikingly at the ranch house.

"I found your note," Buckskin said.

"Good, come sit down over here, we need to talk again."

"You said you wanted to find out who shot your husband. You must know he was shot twice, once with a shotgun, the other time with a handgun of some kind."

"Yes, the undertaker told me that much. I wasn't interested in all the details."

"So which shot do you want to find out about?"

"The handgun one. I want to know who killed my husband."

"I've learned a few things, Mrs. Baines, but that is

not one of them. I know now that your husband had a financial interest in the railroad. He would have been paid what I'd expect was a large sum of money or land for his services. I spoke with the railroad men here from Chicago about an hour ago.

"I also have learned that another man attacked your husband and injured him after the shotgun blast. But this man did not kill your husband."

"Injured him, what do you mean?"

Buckskin looked away and she watched him. At last he turned back to her. "I guess you have a right to know. The undertaker and the doctor confirmed the fact that your husband was castrated some time after he was hit with the shotgun pellets but before he died."

"Oh, my god!" She threw her hands into the air in shock and anger. "Why on earth would anyone want to do that to Elwood?"

"That's another part of this tragedy that may remain a mystery. Doctor Ralston didn't think it should be reported on his death certificate. He wanted to prevent any undue public outcry and the resulting gossip. You asked me, so I felt that I should tell you."

"I can think of one reason someone would castrate a man, but surely—Well, that's something I don't have to be concerned with. I just want to know who fired that handgun."

"I'll tell you when I find out, Mrs. Baines. Now as I remember, our arrangement was for five-thousand dollars for that information. I'm running into some expenses."

"How much expense money do you want?"

"Three hundred dollars will do me for a while."

She looked at him in surprise. "Mr. Morgan. I'm sure you realize that is a lot of money. We hire cowboys for a year out at the ranch for three hundred dollars."

"True, but you give them room and board as well, twenty-five dollars a month and found. I've put in some time in that profession myself, Mrs. Baines. I like my present employment much better."

She stood. Buckskin stood automatically. She smiled. "Mr. Morgan, do you think that I am unattractive?"

"Mrs. Baines, you look a hundred times better now than when I saw you in your grieving period a few days ago. That dress is most becoming."

"You don't think it's too revealing? I mean, shows too much of me in . . . in front?"

"Not at all. In the East the women show much more. Many of the ball gowns are low enough to show cleavage, if I may be so bold as to use the word."

"Yes, you certainly may. Come this way to the den, I'll get you an advance. It's money well spent, and I will give you the five thousand, no matter what name you prove to me was the one who shot my husband."

In the book lined den, Mrs. Baines unlocked a drawer in a massive mahogany desk and took out an envelope. She extracted six $50 bills and counted them twice, then handed them to him.

"There. That should keep you fed and in a hotel room for a few more days. How long do you think it might take to determine for sure who the man was?"

"I'm not sure, Mrs. Baines. I hope less than a week. After a while I'll simply be going over what I already know. I want to fill in the blanks in the puzzle long before then."

"You said you like my dress," she said standing. "Even when I do this?" She twirled around and the dress flared, revealing her legs halfway up her calf.

Buckskin grinned. "Mrs. Baines, I like the dress, especially when you do that."

"Good, would you care to stay and listen to some music on one of those round recording devices that Elwood sent for? Then later we could have supper. I do so dislike eating alone."

Automatically he rejected the idea. She was, in her soft and awkward way, making a play for him. Not yet. The timing wasn't right. He needed to know more about her and about the case. Maybe the next time it would be right and he could ask her about her coffee. Buckskin still considered her an outside suspect in the coffee poisoning.

"That's a tremendously interesting invitation, Mrs. Baines, but I have an appointment for supper and two more people to see this afternoon before then. Maybe we could make it another time?"

She frowned. "Oh, well fine, another time. I was so hoping we could dine together tonight. If you must go, you must. I do expect results for what I'll be paying you."

"Yes, I'll get them for you. Now, I really should be going."

She led him to the front door, holding his arm, pulling herself close against him so his arm brushed her breast. Oh yes, Raquel was ready for a man. He might be able to use that to get the truth out of her about her husband. That is if she really did do him any damage.

She smiled at him when they got to the door.

"You be sure to come back soon so you can keep me up to date on what you find. I'll be living here in town for a while. The children are staying out at the ranch for now."

Morgan nodded, said he'd keep in touch and walked down the path to the street. He still hadn't figured the woman out. She was a direct reversal from the person he had first met at the ranch. Now she was bold, aggressive. Maybe the money and the power did that to a woman.

By the time he made it to Main Street, Buckskin had decided his next stop. Time to talk to the sheriff again. He might have turned up something new. Doubtful, but no sense overlooking any possible help.

Sheriff Jefferson shook his head. "Nope, not a thing. Told you we filed that under the unsolved label. Don't look in them cases again unless something comes up."

"Maybe something did that you didn't know about, Sheriff."

The sheriff heaved his 240 pounds into a more comfortable slouch in his oversized chair behind his desk and scowled. "Something new? What?"

"Elwood Baines was not only shotgunned and head shot, he also was castrated some time between the two shootings. The undertaker and Doc Ralston said they figured it wasn't important at the time of his death to put it in their report, since it didn't have anything to do with the immediate cause of death."

"Castrated? They cut his balls off?"

"Somebody did. Does that interest you at all?"

"Not one hell of a lot. Could have been the same one who fired the fatal shot. He's the man we want, if we can find him. But with no clues to work with, we ain't got one hoot in a holler chance."

Buckskin had not sat down and now he headed for the door. He stopped. "Sheriff, I guess every lawman works a little different. If it was me, I'd think the richest man in the county deserved a little more work at finding out who killed him and why. Could stop a lot of trouble downstream. But, this is your county. There are a few clues around, here and there. I'm finding some, but since you aren't interested, I guess there's no point in telling you about them." He went on to the door.

"Oh, when I find the killer, will it be all right for me to bring him in here for you to arrest?"

Sheriff Jefferson shrugged. "Hell, I don't care. Do with him whatever you want. Figure a trial like that would cost the county near to five-hundred dollars."

Buckskin shook his head and went out. He needed some fresh air.

Back at the hotel, he found no notes in his key box, but a small man in a gray suit and a gray town hat stood from a couch and came forward.

"Mr. Morgan?"

Buckskin stopped. "Could be. Who's asking?"

"I'm Van Taylor. I run a jewelry store down the block. I hear you're the man looking for Elwood Baines' killer. I might have some information that could help you."

"I'm Morgan. What do you know?"

Buckskin looked past the small man and saw Tilly standing there motioning to him. She was shaking her head and pointing to the man in front of him. She motioned again.

"Mr. Morgan, I think I know who killed Mr. Baines. I was just closing up my shop and it was almost dark out. I saw his rig come driving down Main Street. I recognized it because Mr. Baines is, or I guess I should say was, one of my best customers. He drove down Main and stopped down at about third. That's at the end of my block so I could see him easy. One of the girls from the Teton Saloon jumped out of his rig and hurried into the saloon. Sam Talmash, the owner of the place, came racing out as soon as the girl got inside. He ran after the buggy and fired a handgun at the rig four or five times.

"It went bang, bang, then a pause, and bang, bang, bang. Yes, five times. I thought I heard a scream. Then Sam ran down the alley and the buggy kept going but it didn't look like no one was driving the horse, like it was just trotting along, going wherever it wanted to."

Tilly pushed past the small man. "Mr. Morgan. The hotel manager wants to see you right away. He says it's terribly important."

"Yes, thanks. I was just talking to Van here."

"This is more important. He says it can't wait. I'm sure Van can wait a few more minutes for you. Can't you, Van?" Tilly gave him one of her best smiles.

The small man grinned and stepped back.

"This way, Mr. Morgan. I'm sure you'll thank me for what I'm doing."

When they were out of hearing of the small man, Buckskin scowled. "What the hell is this all about?"

"Van Taylor is the biggest liar in town. He tells wild stories about everyone all the time. Nobody believes a word he says. Sorry he trapped you. I do have something to tell you that's important.

"Today I had a message and someone came to see me. She's upstairs in your room right now. I heard she had gone to Omaha, but she hasn't. She goes tomorrow. Irene Channing is up there right now waiting to talk to you. She made me promise to bring you to see her."

Buckskin took the stairs three at a time on his way to the second floor and room 212. He knocked, then opened the door and stepped inside.

A girl stood near the window. She turned and Buckskin saw that she was attractive, not pretty, not plain, but wholesome, and now her face held a sad frown.

"Irene, my name is Lee Morgan. I understand you want to talk to me before you leave tomorrow."

# Chapter Eight

Irene Channing wore a heavy gray dress that draped her frame, concealing what figure she might have. She looked up with sullen eyes.

"I know who you are. I don't like you but I figure I should tell you what happened. My Pa didn't kill Elwood. I guess you know that. Elwood was good to me, made me feel special. My own Pa just yelled at me. Then after you talked to him, he beat me three times."

"I thought you left for Omaha yesterday."

"No. I got on the stage, but had them let me off at the edge of town. Pa said I should. Then he'd hide me for a while. He don't want the whole town to know that I'm pregnant cause that might cause him to lose his church here."

Buckskin made sure the door was closed and that

Tilly had not come inside with him, then he motioned for Irene to sit on the bed. He sat on the chair six feet away.

"You were going to tell me what happened."

"With Elwood? He was a nice man. Treated me like a lady. Made me feel like a woman. He was my first, my very first time. Happened one day when I took some papers to him for Pa. Took them to his town house.

"Elwood invited me in and gave me some lemonade. Then we talked and he told me how pretty I was. Later on that afternoon he bedded me and I liked it and he said we could again sometime. Then pretty soon it was twice a week and I still liked it. He said nothing wrong with us having some fun and doing it that way. I liked it.

"Then one day he said he couldn't see me any more. He said he had a new girl friend, Emmy Lou Henderson. She was only thirteen but had big tits. I know her. I told him he better not touch her or I'd tell Emmy Lou's pa and he'd shoot Elwood deader than a country chicken.

"He just laughed and did me twice that day, then said he didn't believe me. When he was all tired out after the second time, I got his derringer and tried to shoot him, but I pulled the trigger too hard and hit the bed beside him. He took it away from me and twisted my breasts until I screamed. I never tried to shoot him again.

"He never tried to get Emmy Lou's clothes off neither."

"Why did he pick you? Was he coming to you after another girl?"

"I figured so. I asked him, but he wouldn't say. Then three or four times he called me a different name when he was real hot, when he was shooting into me. Called her name a dozen times several different days.

"So I called him on it and he wouldn't say, but I'm sure he'd been poking her all the time before he got to me. She must have cut him off. Yeah, she probably was fearful of getting pregnant. I should have cut him off, too."

"Who was the other girl?"

Irene looked up, her eyes wide with fear for a moment, then they calmed and she shook her head.

"No, I don't think I should tell you."

"Why not? He's dead. You can't hurt Elwood Baines any."

"But the girl ain't dead. Could hurt her considerable."

"Is she pregnant?"

"Nope, I'd guess not."

"But you don't know for sure."

"Yes I know for sure. She's not pregnant. Saw her a couple of days ago."

"Are you glad that Elwood is dead?"

"Oh, god, no. I loved him. He taught me everything. I still love the man."

"Do you want to find out who killed him?"

Her eyes widened and she nodded vigorously. "Oh yes, that's important to me. That's why I asked Tilly to bring me to you."

Buckskin waited a minute. The girl looked up at him. "What can I do to help you find the killer?"

"Were you and the other girl the only ones that

Elwood had played around with?"

"I don't think so, but he never said for sure. He just liked young girls. Said the older women had wrinkles and rolls of fat and they were awkward and they hurt. He liked fresh, young girls he could teach how to make love the way he wanted to."

"I thought one of the other girls' fathers might have found out about Elwood, and instead of just hurting him, shot him, killed him. Do you think that's possible?"

"Not with the last girl before me, but maybe one of the others."

"My problem is I don't know who any of them are. If you could tell me the name of one of them. . . ."

"I only know the one name, the girl just before me."

"Irene, I would appreciate it if you could tell me. It might open up a whole new area for me, get at some information I don't know about and let me find some new suspects."

"Oh." She stood and walked to the window, came back and stood in front of the chair where he sat.

"You wear guns. Have you ever killed anybody?"

"Yes, Irene, I'm afraid I have."

"Oh. What did it feel like?"

"Not good. Not good at all, even if the man I shot deserved to die, would have been hung for his crimes. It still hurts knowing that I've ended another human being's life."

"Then why do you carry the gun?"

"To defend myself. Others enjoy killing, take advantage of people. If I meet one of those men, I want to have an even chance of staying alive."

"Oh." She went back to the window and looked down on the street. "Lots of people down there. I'm gonna birth a new one into that whole world of humans. A brand new life. I can't get over the thrill of it. Course I wish I had me a husband and he had a good job and we had a house and—"

"Irene. It would be a great help to me if you would tell me who Elwood Baines was having sexual relations with before you went to his house that day."

She sighed and turned around. "It will put him in a bad light if it gets out. You got to promise you won't tell nobody, nobody at all."

"I promise."

She came back toward him and stared hard at him. "Elwood Baines was a fine man. He had a crazy woman for a wife. He had need for a woman and she pushed him out of her bedroom. For a while he said he went to the whores, but they didn't really satisfy him. Before me, he had been having sex with his daughter, Midge."

"My god. Then that's why—" It hit him hard. A man taking advantage of his fifteen year old daughter. He might have been at her when she was fourteen or even thirteen. My God! How could a man do that to his own daughter?

"You're sure it was Midge he was involved with, not a name that sounded like that?"

"Oh, no, it was Midge. We even talked about it. He swore me to secrecy. He said it happened accidentally, then neither of them could stop it."

"Who finally put an end to it?"

"Midge did. She had a derringer he had given her and she threatened him with it. He left and went to town and used the fancy ladies for a week, then I stopped by at his house with the papers from Pa."

"I'm sorry you were in the middle of all of this mixed up tragedy, Irene."

She pondered that a minute. "Really, I'm not all that sorry. I wish I hadn't got pregnant, but nobody told me how not to. I couldn't even ask anyone. But those were some of the best days I've ever had. I looked forward to Tuesday and Thursday."

"What will you do now?"

"Oh, I'll go to Omaha, eventually, but not to go to school. My Aunt Martha isn't what you'd call a friendly person. She'll work my tail off for the next three or four months. I'll have the baby and give her up to someone, then come home. Or maybe just stay in Omaha. Get a job. Lots of jobs for girls in Omaha without laying on your back."

Buckskin grinned. "At least you've ruled that out."

"Yeah. I'll get by."

"Irene, I think you will. Thanks for helping me. Now I have another chance to find the killer. I appreciate it."

"Good. I better get back home before Pa misses me. I'm not even supposed to be here. I went out on the stage in the morning all dressed up like a little old lady with the vapors."

Buckskin opened the door and she looked out, saw the hall was clear and then headed for the back stairs. As soon as she vanished down them, Tilly came around the corner and marched to his room.

"So?"

"True, you were right, she wanted to see me."

"Hey, what did she tell you? Was she getting poked

by Baines? She must have loved it. Twice a week? Every day? How often?"

They stepped inside his room and Tilly closed the door and turned the key, then brought it back halfway so it couldn't be pushed out of the lock from the outside.

When she stepped back to him she grinned. "Come on, tell me all the juicy details or I just might never let you touch me again."

"Is that right?" Buckskin put his arms around her and kissed her mouth, which came open and sucked in his tongue. She whimpered and ground her crotch against his. He held the kiss a long time, then let her go and she took three big breaths.

"Oh damn. I don't care if I ever know what she told you. All I want right now is right here."

She knelt in front of him and kissed his pants over his fly where a large bulge was growing. "Yes, yes." She worked feverishly to unbutton the fasteners and to work through to his flesh. A few moment later she had his erection pulled out of his pants.

"The most beautiful sight in the whole fucking world," Tilly said. She leaned forward and kissed the purple head and it jerked in anticipation. Tilly grinned and did it again and then a third time. She spread her kisses down the shank to the hairy roots and then back up.

Buckskin stood there with his legs spread, holding onto the headboard to keep his balance.

Tilly slid her lips around the arrow head of his erection and pulled half of it into her mouth. Her teeth nibbled at the hardness, then she sucked and bobbed back and forth.

Buckskin let out a soft moan of rapture and Tilly came off him and grinned. "Hey, I think you better sit down on the bed before you fall down. Just back up and sit down and keep your knees spread wide. I need room to work."

Buckskin sat down, then pulled her up and kissed her lips.

"You don't have to."

She laughed. "Damn right I don't have to. Sometimes I go just wild for the chance to suck a big cock like this, and this is the day."

She grinned and went down on him again, sucking and bouncing and with one hand playing with his pulled up tight scrotum, massaging his balls with gentle fingers and burning his fires higher and brighter.

Buckskin closed his eyes and put his hands in her hair and held on. She bobbed another dozen times and he knew he was on the way. Her mouth worked its magic on him. He was closer, closer.

She pulled off him, lay on her back on the bed and urged him to come up to her with his knees around her chest. She pulled down his erection and took it in her mouth again.

Buckskin found the new position better. He stroked gently with his hips. She took it, almost gagged, then caught the shaft with her hand so he couldn't get in too far. He found an easy rhythm and stroked again and again.

She mewed at him and her other hand found his swinging scrotum and massaged him gently.

It was more than he could stand. His hips shot forward and he bellowed in victory as he powered into her again and again until he was dry and she sucked at him, cleaning him with her tongue until he began to soften. Then she pulled away and pushed him down so he could lie on top of her as his breath came like a laboring steam engine, decreasing gradually until he could breathe normally.

"Wonderful," she said softly.

"Marvelous," he said.

He revived and rolled them over with her on top of him and stared at her. "You're going to wear me down to a nub, you know that?"

She grinned and kissed him. "It will take a lot of wearing down, but I'm willing to try three or four times a day if you are."

He kissed her again and chuckled. "You are an absolute crazy woman, and I love it."

"Good. What did Irene tell you?"

"I can't tell you. I promised her."

"So break a promise. She won't even be here. She'll be growing a kid in her belly in Omaha."

"Would you want me to break a promise to you?"

"Hell yes, if it was as wild as this bit of information might be. Was my getting Irene here for you helpful? Will it help you find the killer?"

"It might. All along I've been hunting two killers."

"That can't be. How can a body get killed twice?"

"Not easy, but it can happen. Let's say I shoot somebody and he's losing so much blood he'll die in ten minutes. Somebody else comes along and ties the same man to the train tracks and the train runs over him and cuts him in half. Who killed him?"

"The last one, the train did it."

"But I figured I'd killed him. My bullet would have

if the others hadn't messed into the affair."

"Would have, would have. I still think you only have one killer."

"Maybe. What time is it?"

She shrugged so he dug into his pocket for his Waterbury and read the time of day. It was ten minutes past five.

"Will the dining room send dinner up to my room?" he asked.

"Sure. Charge twice as much, but they'll have someone, probably me, bring it up."

"Good. Order us two steaks, mine blood rare, however you want yours. Dinners." He handed her a five dollar gold piece. "Pay for them and bring them up. Then we'll eat and then figure out what to do for an encore, only next time we'll have our clothes off."

It was nearly half an hour later when she brought the two steak dinners upstairs on a large tray and set it on the bed. They sat cross-legged on the bed and ate. The steak was good and Buckskin enjoyed it. He also enjoyed the view as Tilly tipped up her crossed legs now and then, inviting him to peek under her dress.

"You're a tease," he said.

"You bet. Usually it works."

Buckskin enjoyed the rare steak. The side dishes were good too and when he finished he turned and stretched out on the big bed. A moment later Tilly slid over and moved the tray to the floor, then lowered herself delicately on top of him.

"Almost time for a shoot-out," Tilly said.

"You want to be the good girl or the bad girl?"

"Do both of them get shot?"

"Of course."

"Then I want to be the bad girl. They always have the most fun."

It was nearly two o'clock in the morning before the shootout finished and by then both of them were so tired they could barely slip under the sheet and find the pillows.

For just a moment Buckskin planned out the next day. He would go out to the ranch and confront Midge about having been sexually abused by her father. There were laws against such acts, but the law could have little effect now with Baines dead. Would it be of any benefit to the girl or the community to make such behavior public?

Tilly revived for a minute and held out a note. "Oh, somebody put this in your box and I slipped it out but forgot to give it to you. Hope it's important."

He read the note inside a sealed envelope. It was from Gretchen, the madam at the whorehouse.

"Morgan. Found out who the man was who talked about Elwood Baines being castrated. He was the undertaker, Horatio Weaver. Hope this helps. Come see us for business!"

"Important?" a sleepy Tilly asked. He kissed her and told her not that important and she nodded and went to sleep.

No help from the whores. Buckskin decided he'd have to play it as it came, but right then he figured he'd keep quiet about the incest unless it would do him some good somewhere. Buckskin sighed, fondled Tilly's breasts. She smiled in her sleep. He closed his eyes and let blessed unconsciousness overtake him.

# Chapter Nine

Tilly was gone when Buckskin awoke at 6:30 the next morning. He stretched, washed up, shaved in cold water and put on his semi-town clothes. A clean pair of pants, a blue shirt with long sleeves and the tan leather vest.

He had breakfast at the Grand Teton Cafe and told Josh Baines about his brother's connection with the railroad men.

"I figure he was in line to take in a big pile of cash or land for providing the rails smooth sailing through the county and into town," Buckskin said. "Somehow I have a feeling that might be a motive for murder. Of course, then someone else would have to be in line to take over the contact job here."

"Looks like Adler Pickering already done that," Josh said between flipping eggs on the grill. "He met them three yesterday and spent most of the day with them at his office. They had supper in here and then went straight to the hotel. Figure they'll be on the morning stage."

"I talked to the four of them yesterday in Pickering's office," Buckskin said. "The gents from Chicago didn't look like killers."

"These days, how can you tell?" Josh said and put up three plates of eggs, sausages, pancakes and country fries.

Buckskin considered that as he finished his own breakfast, a logger's feast he called it with lots of food. He left without talking to Josh again and headed for the livery stable. He needed a horse for the three mile ride out to the Baines Box B ranch house.

His first order of business was to find Midge and talk with her like a prosecuting attorney. He'd scare her if he had to, threaten to spread the whole ugly affair in the *Jackson Hole Tribune* for everyone to see. He had just come around the edge of the livery when a revolver shot slammed into the morning stillness and red hot lead ripped into his left leg, staggering him but not knocking him down.

He saw wisps of white smoke at the far edge of the livery and put two rounds into the corner of the wood as he ran that way. He had drawn and fired automatically, the way he always did when someone attacked him. Now he edged around the wooden corner with his bullet holes in it and saw a gray horse pounding away from him past the fenced pasture and into the open country out of town.

The pain washed over him and he knew he'd been hit in the leg. He wasn't sure how high the wound was, but he could still walk and run. Buckskin raced back to the livery door, saw a horse saddled and waiting and jumped on it. The livery man came out, screeching at him that the horse was for someone else, but Buckskin didn't have time to argue. He pulled the mount's head around and kicked her in the flanks as he rode hard for the edge of the livery and looked ahead for the gray. He saw it just disappearing from sight into a small depression.

Now he could feel blood running down his leg and pooling in his boot. He'd have to tie up that wound soon or it wouldn't matter if he caught the bushwhacker or not.

He pounded up the gentle rise until he could see the gray ahead of him about a quarter of a mile. There was a long level area ahead of the other rider two miles wide. Buckskin pulled his mount to a halt and lifted his left leg to the front of the saddle horn.

The blood smear on his leg was high up on the outside of his thigh. He dropped off the horse, blanched at the pain in his leg when his feet hit the ground, and sat down and pulled down his pants. The slug had cut through about midway up his thigh, digging through an inch of flesh and exiting, leaving a nasty hole with blood draining out. He took two handkerchiefs from his pocket and tied the corners together.

With his knife he cut off the tail of his shirt to form two pads. He held them in place and tied the handkerchiefs firmly around his leg to keep the pads over the bullet holes. That would stop the bleeding.

He took a moment to get back on his horse. The leg would hurt and hinder him, but he had to catch the man who fired at him. He looked ahead. The gray was another quarter of a mile away. It had slowed to a walk and worked toward Flat Creek and its broad valley. Soon the horseman turned to the east and aimed at timber covered hills that worked into the higher mountains behind them. Where was he going?

Buckskin kicked his mount into a canter and then galloped her for a quarter of a mile, reducing the distance between the two men to four-hundred yards. Then Buckskin eased off and kept his mount at a fast walk.

He had thought of pushing his animal and galloping until he caught the other rider, but his horse could burn out and go down if he pushed her too hard. Better to play it safe and work at closing the gap to a practical distance, then making a run at the other rider.

That would trigger the other one to gallop as well. What it could come down to was a long chase unless one of the horses was in much better condition and faster than the other one. Even as he thought about it, Buckskin realized the other rider was slowly creeping away from him.

Buckskin kicked his mount into a canter to close the distance, but the rider ahead copied the tactic and stayed well out in front.

After a half hour of riding, the shock wore off and his leg hurt like raw fire in the wound. He tried to put it out of his mind. How could he overtake this rider?

The lead rider turned again, this time into a small valley between hills that rose on either side to eight-hundred feet over the valley floor. The hills on both sides were heavily timbered with ponderosa pine and a sprinkling of Englemann spruce. The edges of the valley held clusters of quaking aspen and a few cottonwood.

Halfway up the valley, the bushwhacker turned into the quaking aspen and vanished. Four-hundred yards behind the runner, Buckskin stopped. It was the perfect setup for an ambush. If he rode into the same spot where the gunman vanished, the man could be waiting a dozen feet away and blast him with five rounds from his six-gun.

Buckskin had been this route before. He rode to within fifty yards of the spot where the bushwhacker vanished. That was well out of good revolver range. There he rode into the trees and brush. The aspen faded quickly and he rode through a pine forest with few small trees and little underbrush. Now he could see another fifty yards ahead in most places.

Buckskin stopped his mount and listened. He could hear the blowing of a horse ahead, and the creak of leather. The sound came from the right and up the slope of the mountain. He kicked his horse into motion and rode as fast as the animal could along the sloping rise of the mountain.

Fifty yards ahead he stopped again and listened. This time he heard nothing. He waited. Two long minutes later he heard a horseshoe click on rocks in the loose forest mulch. The sounds came now from the left and downhill.

He took a chance and charged downhill and to the left, smashing through light growth, surging around trees. Ahead he saw a flash of horseflesh before it vanished into some small quaking aspen. He drew his six-gun and charged ahead. Once through the next screen-

ing of brush he caught sight of the bushwhacker. He
was no more than thirty yards in front.

Buckskin took a shot. The man turned, fear on his
face, and kicked his mount in the sides and plunged
harder down the slope. Buckskin's shot missed. He
continued the chase. Ahead he heard a scream, then
the piercing cry of a wounded horse.

He slowed his mount and edged through another
curtain of heavy brush and small aspen. In a heartbeat,
he stopped the mount and jerked it backwards. Just in
front of him, the ground fell away into a forty foot
deep canyon. It looked as if the earth had simply split
apart and dropped away. He swung off the horse and
crept to the edge of the chasm.

Below he saw the horse sprawled in the dust and
rocks of the floor of the ravine. It pawed the ground
with its two back feet, screamed again in that high,
piercing cry and then lay still.

Where was the rider?

Buckskin scanned the ravine's sides. It was almost
a straight drop. There was no human body below in
the wash. He pushed out farther and checked the near
side of the ditch. He saw a quaking aspen bent double
and angled down the side of the cut. It was a four-inch-
thick tree that had been bent over by some great force,
perhaps the horse's weight smashing it forward as the
animal fell.

He frowned, then looked again at the leafy form of
the tree halfway down the embankment. Some of the
leaves moved. Then the whole top of the tree quivered
and trembled. He saw why they called them quaking
aspens. Every leaf on the tree fluttered as if it was in
a windstorm.

117

A darker blob showed under the leaves. Then he saw an arm appear and grab the branches as a man worked his way down the top branches of the slender tree toward the bottom of the ravine. Even from the end of the bent over tree there would be a fifteen foot fall to the bottom of the canyon.

Buckskin put a .45 slug into the tree behind the man and shouted.

"That's far enough. Move another inch downward and I'll cut you in half with forty-five slugs."

Instead of stopping, the figure turned and fired at Buckskin who had to drop to the ground and scurry behind some cover. When he looked over the side again, the man was at the end of the tree branches. He dropped to the side of the ravine and rolled and tumbled another ten feet to the bottom.

Buckskin fired again and saw the round hit the man in the leg before he could crawl behind a large boulder that completely hid him.

The big detective considered his situation. The bushwhacker was afoot and wounded. Buckskin was wounded but still had his horse. The advantage was his. All he had to do was ride along the top of the slice through the mountain, following the bushwhacker until he tried to climb out. The contest should go to Buckskin

It worked that way for two-hundred yards. The depth of the slice through the mountain became deeper as it worked down the slope. Soon it was sixty feet to the bottom, then seventy feet. When the slice came to the smaller hills and then the open valley, it would become shallower until it emptied onto the valley floor.

That's the way it should have worked. Fifty yards downstream of the ravine, it split and a second ravine branched off to the left, away from Buckskin. He had been watching the man move along the gully floor below. Buckskin had decided not to kill him but to find out first who he was and why he had tried to kill Buckskin. Now the man looked back where he had last seen Buckskin and hurried down the split of the ravine to the left.

Soon the man would be out of sight. Buckskin swore, kicked off the horse, tied her reins back on the saddlehorn so she could wander where she wanted to, and eyed the ravine slope. Somehow he had to get down there. To his relief he saw that the sides were now sharply sloped, but at least not a sheer dropoff. Buckskin knew it would be a miracle if he could walk down the side without falling. But he had to try.

He picked the best route, going at an angle down the side to reduce his chance of falling. The first one-third of the slope went easily, then he twisted his ankle on a rock in the slope, felt it turn and upset his balance.

He plunged to the left to hit the bank, then he slid directly down the slope on his britches, feet first. One boot caught on a rock, twisting him sideways. He rolled and tumbled. He still had the .45 in his hand and clutched it to his chest as he ducked his head to keep from bashing his brains out on another rock outcropping.

In twenty seconds he stopped at the bottom. Buckskin coughed to get the dust out of his nose and mouth, then he sat up and examined his body. His left leg hurt like fire again. He still had the .45 Colt in his firm right hand and he had a long gash on his left hand and up his arm. It bled but not dangerously.

With a great effort he got to his knees and then stood.

Good, no broken bones. He shook the dust off his clothes, found his hat a dozen feet downstream and jammed it on his head. Holding the six-gun at the ready, he ran fifty feet back the way they had come to where the ravine parted.

Just as Buckskin came around the branch in the ditch, the bushwhacker fired at him twice from behind some rocks ahead. Buckskin dove to the ground and worked behind a small boulder that would protect only half his body.

No more shots came. Buckskin looked out and saw the man in the brown jacket racing away from him.

Buckskin jumped to his feet, pushed a sixth round into his weapon and ran after the man ahead. The bushwhacker was about forty yards in front of him now. The gully was almost flat on the bottom with few rocks along here. Evidently it was a wash where cloudbursts in the mountains sent a boiling flood down the slopes toward the Snake River.

He tried to increase his speed but his leg hurt like a hot poker had seared his flesh. Every step now was a painful one, but he had to run, had to catch this man who might know about who killed Baines. He had reasoned it out on the chase. He had no enemies in town—except the man who had killed Elwood Baines. The man who shot at him must be in on that conspiracy somehow. He simply could not let him get away.

Buckskin felt blood running down his leg again. The fall must have knocked the bandage off and opened the wounds. No time to tend to it now.

He set his jaw, squinted and ran ahead, battering down the pain, watching for a chance to get off a shot to bring the man down.

Ahead, he saw his target stumble over a rock in the wash and go down hard. He struggled to a sitting position, pulled out his six-gun and fired. The round came close. Buckskin didn't want to kill him. He didn't have much of a target but he aimed for the man's gunhand shoulder and fired. He missed.

The bushwhacker struggled up and ran, but now he limped badly.

Buckskin saw his advantage and spurted ahead, gaining rapidly. The man didn't look back. When he was twenty yards from the other man, Buckskin stopped running and fired. His round bored home, slamming into the runner's left leg, buckling it, sprawling the man in the dirt and making him drop his gun which clattered away three feet from his outstretched hand.

Buckskin moved up cautiously. The bushwhacker could have a hide-out derringer.

"Don't move or you're a dead man," Buckskin barked. He walked up carefully, kicked the six-gun farther away and turned to face the runner.

He was Adler Pickering, the lawyer, the man who was trying to take Elwood Baines' place with the Chicago railmen.

"Pickering, I might have known. Why did you kill Elwood Baines?"

"I don't know what you're talking about."

"Oh, but you do. You found him in the buggy when it came down Main. Saw that he was bleeding from his legs. You turned the rig around and took it out of town, planted his own derringer at the back of his head and fired the fatal bullet."

"You must have some strong evidence, some proof to support a statement like that. I'm a lawyer, where are your facts, your proof?"

"I won't need any except your confession."

Pickering laughed, then winced as he moved his leg. Buckskin pulled his own pants down and checked his leg wound. The pads had shifted but were still there. Only one of the bullet holes had broken open. He adjusted the pads, retied the handkerchiefs to hold them in place and pulled his pants back in place.

"Come on, Morgan. Where's your proof? What are you going to show the judge or even the district attorney?"

"Your confession. I see you're wearing town shoes. Not good for this kind of country. Take them off."

"What?"

"I said, take off your shoes and stockings."

"I'll do no such thing."

The slug from Buckskin's Colt buried itself in the sand an inch from Pickering's right shoe. The sound of the shot echoed off and down the ravine.

"What the hell?"

"The next one goes in your right leg. You want three bullet holes in you leaking blood?"

Slowly the lawyer took off his shoes and stockings.

"Toss them over here."

The man did as instructed. "Now, if you're through playing games, it's time you tied up my wounds. I'm bleeding too much."

"Do it yourself," Buckskin said.

"What? I can't. I don't know how. They hurt too much."

"Take off your jacket," Buckskin said.

"Why?"

Buckskin cocked his six-gun. Pickering shucked out of the brown jacket and tossed it where he had put the shoes.

"Now, did you kill Baines just to get the contact with the railroad men?"

"I don't have to answer any questions."

"True. Take off your pants."

"What?"

Buckskin brought the Colt down and aimed it at Pickering's right thigh. The thin man in the black suit sighed and unbuckled his belt. He lifted off the sand just enough to pull his pants off his hips, then down and off his legs. He threw them on the pile of clothes.

Buckskin stood and checked the wash. A few rocks here along the far side. There probably had been water there. He found a sturdy stick that had washed down and began turning over the foot-wide flat rocks. He found what he wanted on the fifth rock.

The diamond-back rattlesnake blinked in the suddenly bright sun, then started to coil, but instead slid away to the left. Buckskin brought the side of the stick down across the snake an inch behind its head to hold it tightly to the ground, then grabbed the threshing tail and held the three-foot long rattler by the tail at arm's length and walked back to where Pickering had been watching him.

"Well, I found a little friend of yours, Pickering. It's used in an interesting kind of Indian justice. My

Cheyenne friends say that the rattler is their friend. They never kill a snake. They use them in some of their justice rituals. Works like this. They tie a snake by the tail with a rawhide thong and give it enough length so it can crawl to the accused man. If the rattler strikes and kills the brave, then he was guilty.

"If the rattler ignores the man tied to the ground in front of him and goes back the other way, the man is innocent and released. I can't say for sure if the story is true or not, but it's worth a try. No, no, you just sit still. I've got an old bootlace in my pocket that will work for the rawhide strip. I'll just hold you in place so we don't have to tie you down."

Buckskin found a stick he could drive into the sandy soil with a rock. Then he tied the tail of the rattler with the three foot long boot lace and knotted the other end to the stake in the sand. He let the rattler crawl back and forth and eventually marked a circle of the farthest points he could reach.

Then Buckskin went to Pickering. "Stand up and walk up there toward the snake. Hell, we'll let him see if he likes your toes or your ankles. That'll be enough to establish your proof or guilt."

"Oh, damn. I hate snakes! Not a chance I'm going to let you do this."

"Hey, don't worry. If the snake goes the other way, I take you in to Doc Ralston and I pay his fee for patching you up. You're in the clear. Come on now, stand up so I don't have to carry you."

Pickering edged backwards in the sand away from the rattlesnake ten feet away.

"I said no."

Buckskin grabbed the thin man and lifted him to his feet, then kicked the back of his ankles gently until he walked forward. Buckskin walked him around until he was on the other side of the circle from the snake. He moved him in a foot from the farthest the snake could reach which would give the reptile enough space to make one coil so it could strike.

It took ten minutes before the snake sensed the hated human smell across the circle. It coiled and rattled, then uncoiled and slithered directly across the circle at Pickering.

The lawyer screamed and took a step backwards. Buckskin tapped his achilles tendons and he moved back in place. The rattler came closer. It stopped three-feet away, testing the air with its forked tongue. Then satisfied, it moved forward.

"God, no! Let me out of here." Pickering surged backwards, caught Buckskin unprepared and bowled him over. They both fell to the ground away from the snake. Buckskin rolled on top of the thin man, put his knees on his chest and pushed his Colt's muzzle under the lawyer's chin.

"I'd say the rattler would have struck you half a dozen times, Pickering. Tell me about it. You knew Baines was coming to town that night to get his Chicago letters because you sent a note to the ranch, right?"

Pickering nodded.

"You waited for his rig, almost missed it because somebody else got to him first. You were surprised by the bloody legs and bloody crotch. He was half out of his mind by then with the pain, right? Was he still unconscious?"

"No, but he was blubbering like an idiot. He couldn't talk."

"So you drove him out of town aways, found his own derringer in the seat and shot him with it. Right?"

"Yes, yes! Just don't make me go back by that snake."

"You knew how much Baines was getting to help the railroad men, correct?"

"Yes. He was getting fifty-thousand in cash and the deeds to two-hundred square miles of railroad land grants near town, much of it good land. Now can we get to the doctor?"

"Why did you hate him so much?"

"Because I was getting just five-thousand dollars for my part in the railroad deal. I did all of the work. I contacted the people. It was just his name. I deserved the money."

"So you planned to kill him. You met him, you drove him out of town, and you killed him."

"Whoever used that shotgun almost beat me to it. What I couldn't figure out was why he was babbling. He couldn't talk plain. His eyes were rolled back in his head, he was breathing funny."

Buckskin backed away from the killer. "That was because somebody had poisoned him less than an hour before you shot him. Seems a lot of folks wanted Elwood Baines dead."

"Poisoned him? You mean if I hadn't shot him, he would have died anyway?"

"Right, and you would have still gotten the railroad deal. Now, it doesn't look like you'll live long enough to see the rails come to Jackson. I've heard this county has a swift justice court and a fine hangman."

"No! No, I won't let you take me back. I'll run until I drop. You'll have to shoot me to stop me."

"You don't have any shoes or pants on, Pickering."

"You won't be able to stop me."

He faced Buckskin and took two steps backward, then another one. Buckskin watched his face. He was serious. The man took another step back, then he screamed. He looked down and saw he had stepped on the tail of the rattler. It coiled and struck his foot before he could move it. It struck again, and a third time. Pickering screamed and fell.

Buckskin had his six-gun out and fired twice, but not before the furious snake had struck two more times, sinking its fangs into Pickering's bare thigh and pumping the deadly venom into his flesh.

The rattler jolted to the side as one of the .45 rounds tore off half of its head and slammed it back to the stake where its tail remained tied. Buckskin knelt beside the lawyer, his face pale, his breath coming in quick gasps.

"Help me, Morgan! Help me! Damned snake bit me five or six times. Help me!"

The last came as a scream and Pickering's head sagged to the ground, his shoulders slumped and a last gush of deadly air came from his lungs.

Buckskin checked for a pulse, then for breathing. The Jackson lawyer was dead. The snake poison hadn't killed him. There hadn't been time enough for that. He had died of fear and shock from the rattlesnake bites. His heart couldn't take the strain. Buckskin untied the boot lace from the rattler's tail, pulled up the stake from the sand and threw it down the wash, but left the dead snake there. No sense leaving anything for the sheriff to ask questions about.

It was past noon when Buckskin crawled up the ravine's bank and walked back to the spot where he had left his horse. The animal had found some fresh grass and was munching away contentedly when Buckskin walked up to her.

He mounted and rode back to town. He told the sheriff about his bushwhacking wound, his chase and the demise of the lawyer. Sheriff Jefferson harumphed, said he knew about the canyon and sent two deputies and three horses to get the body.

"I suppose this has something to do with the Baines killing," Sheriff Jefferson said.

"It does. Pickering confessed to shooting Baines so he could get the inside track with the railroad men who were in town yesterday. I'd say I can't prove it in court, but there won't be any need for that since my bullets didn't kill him. I'll write out a complete report for your file just as soon as I have time. I'm going to get a big dinner, then go calling."

The sheriff frowned. "Calling? On who?"

"First on the sawbones to bind up my wounds. Then I'm going calling on a lady, Sheriff, on a young lady."

# Chapter Ten

Doc Ralston clucked at Buckskin's leg wounds and the dirt that had filtered into them. He washed them out with something that made the leg hurt more than it had the first time. He bandaged up the thigh and put a small bandage on Buckskin's arm and hand, then sent him on his way.

Buckskin had kept the horse he used that morning, so he mounted and rode the three miles to the Baines Box B ranch house. He fully expected Midge to be home. She'd have the big house to herself most of the time now with her mother in town.

Midge answered the back door when he knocked. Nobody seemed to be around the barns or corral. All out on the range getting the work done, Buckskin decided.

Midge pushed open the door and grinned. "Good,

129

you've come back. I didn't scare you away the other day."

"Why on earth would I be frightened? May I come in?"

She waved him into the kitchen.

"You want to talk here or up in my bedroom?"

"Here will be fine. You have any coffee on the back lid?"

The coffee was cold so she started a fire and moved the pot of java to the front of the stove.

"I wanted to talk to you about your father, and a girl in town. Do you know Irene Channing?"

"The P.K.? Sure I know her. She's two years older than me. I used to see her in school sometimes." Midge frowned. "You don't mean that Irene—" Midge giggled. "Irene and my father. Now there's a picture. Of course I remember Irene. She didn't know she had tits for a year after they began to grow. When she got her period you would have thought the world had come to an end. She honestly thought she was bleeding to death."

"Irene is leaving town today. Going to Omaha to further her education and live with her aunt."

Midge laughed and pushed another stick into the kitchen range fire box.

"Sure she is, further her education about how to be a mother and let her little bastard grow in her belly. We've all heard those stories about girls going away to school. That's a real laugh with Irene. I heard somebody planted a seed in her belly. She was plain dumb in school. Took her a year longer than the rest of us to learn to read. She never did catch up.

"Damn, I just can't imagine Pa with her, both of

130

them naked in the town house and him up there on top of her skinny little form just pumping away. Damn but that sounds weird."

"I talked to Irene yesterday. She said she got involved with your father accidentally, then it became a regular thing."

"Oh, yeah. Pa liked to get a poking at least twice a week."

"Irene said she still loves him. That he was good to her."

"Why not? He was fucking up a storm with her and not getting caught. He should have been delighted. Pa liked to take whatever he wanted."

"Irene said your father came to her after he'd been cut off by somebody else. She said he tried the whores in town for a week and couldn't take them anymore."

"Irene said some woman cut off my father? Wouldn't let him poke her anymore?"

"That's what she said."

Midge looked a little uncomfortable for the first time. She tested the coffee, yelped when it burned her finger and poured them two cups which she set on the kitchen table. She slid onto the wooden bench and stared at Buckskin.

"Did Irene say who this woman was who cut Pa off from getting his balls popped?"

"Yes she did. She said it was you."

Midge lifted her brows and sighed. "Well, Irene was right. It wasn't anything he planned. He told me that."

"How long, Midge?"

"Hell, since I was thirteen. I developed early. Had

131

big tits when I was twelve and a half. Then before I
was thirteen I got my period and I had all these hot
spells when I really wanted to know about boys, men.

"Once I heard the bed springs squeaking upstairs
and I went down the hall quietly to investigate. The
door was open to the spare bedroom and when I
peeked in I saw two naked bodies just humping away
like crazy on the bed. It was Pa and the woman cook
we had for a while. I watched as they both cum and
then I slipped away and bolted my door. I took off all
my clothes and stared at my naked body. I wanted
somebody to do that to me."

"But you didn't approach anyone."

"Of course not, I was only thirteen. It would have
embarrassed me to death to even go out to the bunkhouse. Well, about a month later, I was just getting
out of my bath and I had reached for a towel when Pa
backed into the bathroom and pulled out his whanger
looking for the white chamber.

"I was so surprised I dropped the towel. Pa turned
around and saw me and let out a little cry. Then he
walked up to me and stared. When I didn't move he
began to touch me all over and before I knew it I was
breathing hard and I wanted more than anything in the
world to know how it felt to have his big thing deep
inside me.

"So that was the first time, right there in the bathroom. Two nights later he came into my bedroom and
he showed me everything about his body, and told me
what was happening, and how not to be afraid, and we
did it again.

"I was thrilled and scared to death. He said not to
tell anyone, it was our secret forever."

"But then about six months ago you cut him off, right?"

"Yes. I told him I was afraid of getting pregnant. I was too young to get married and I hadn't had any boyfriends. How could I do it? He agreed not to bed me anymore.

"So he didn't. Every night when he left for town he'd look at me but I'd shake my head when Ma couldn't see me and he'd storm out of the house. Then he calmed down and I knew he was getting somebody regular. That made me jealous. If I couldn't have him, why should some slut in town use him? I was just plain jealous."

"Midge, there's something else you should know. Before your father died, the Preacher Channing caught him and castrated him for making Irene pregnant."

Midge shook her head. "Nobody should do that to my Pa. I won't let them do that. I hate you for telling me about that."

She ran to the closet near the kitchen's outside door and pulled out a sawed off shotgun and made sure both barrels were loaded. Then she aimed the weapon at Buckskin. "Nobody talks about my Pa that way."

"Hey, easy. I'm just telling you what Dwight Channing told me he did. He's the one you need to point that shotgun at, not me. You understand that?"

Her eyes glazed over for a minute and she lifted the weapon. But when he bellowed her name, she jolted back a step, shook her head and stared at him. She lowered the shotgun and shrugged. "I just kind of went wild there for a minute. Sorry."

"Was that the same thing you did the night your father died? You have a shotgun. Did you shoot at your pa that same night he never came home?"

"No, of course not. Why would I want to do that?"

Buckskin walked toward her slowly, showing no anger or indications that he was upset. He reached her and took the shotgun from her hands.

"You said you were jealous of the woman your father had in town. Tell me what happened that night. You knew he was going to town to get some poking, didn't you?"

Midge nodded.

"That made you angry, right?"

Midge looked at him. "Yes, it made me terribly angry."

"So what did you do when you knew your pa was going to town to see some woman?"

"I got my shotgun and went a hundred yards or so down the lane, down there where the trees come over from the river. I waited for him. It was a warm evening, so I took off my blouse and my chemise and waited for him.

"Wasn't near dark when he came down the lane in the buggy. I walked out in the lane so he could see me and he came up and stopped. He always liked my titties. He asked me what I was doing and I told him waiting for him. I wanted him again, just like old times.

"He grinned and said he figured he could spare me one poking and stepped down from the buggy and walked toward me. I'd held the shotgun behind my skirt with one hand and then I lifted it and he laughed. He told me not a chance in the world I would pull the trigger.

"That made me as mad as his having another woman, so I pulled the trigger. But I'm not real good with a shotgun. I aimed too low and most of the shot went into the ground, but lots hit him in the legs and knocked him down. I wanted to use the other barrel and finish him, but at the last minute he screamed in pain and I couldn't. I saw him get up and stagger back to the buggy so I ran for the house and put the shotgun away."

She leaned toward Buckskin and he put his arm around her.

She looked up and wiped tears from her eyes. "Buckskin, did I kill my own father?"

He explained to her that the shot up legs hadn't been what caused her father's death. It made her feel a little better. She recovered more and sipped at her coffee, then stared at him.

"Buckskin, will you stay here with me tonight? I need somebody. I need somebody to hold me and to love me and tell me that I'm not all bad. There must be some good parts to me somewhere. Can you do that? I'd appreciate it just ever so much."

"I'd like to, Midge. But I just can't. I've got to get back to town and talk to a few more people. I did find out who killed your father. Do you want to know who it was?"

"Yes, I do want to know. For quite a while there I thought I might have been the one."

"It was his lawyer, Adler Pickering. He wanted the money the railroad men were going to pay your father. You are convinced now that you didn't kill your father?"

"Yes, I'm sure of it now."

"Oh, one more question. Were you here for supper

the night before your father went to town that last time?"

"Yes."

"Did your father drink any coffee that night?"

"He always has at least two cups. I don't like coffee, and that night my mother said she was going to have some hot tea just for a change."

"Thanks, Midge. Now, I want you to find a good book, have a nice hot bath and get relaxed. Then read the book until you fall asleep. Can you do that?"

She said she would and kissed him on the cheek. Buckskin left the kitchen, found his horse and rode back toward Jackson. He was going to have an interesting meeting with the widow Baines. Had she or had she not poisoned the coffee she fed to her husband his last night on earth?

Buckskin got back to town about three that afternoon and went directly to the sheriff's office. He wanted to write out a deposition on the death of lawyer Adler Pickering and have that wrapped up and finished. Then he'd approach the widow Baines for her rendition of the last supper for Elwood Baines.

The big detective tied his horse up outside the courthouse and walked into the sheriff's office. He heard a gasp when he stepped into the room, then looked up to see two shotguns aimed at him held by deputy sheriffs.

"Afternoon, gentlemen. You practicing some kind of weapons use on bank robbers?"

Sheriff Fillmore Jefferson came out of his office with his six-gun out and cocked.

"Afraid we're not on any kind of drill, Morgan. Raise your hands slowly and put them on the counter there, then lean over and stretch back as far as you can go. You're under arrest for the murder of Adler Pickering."

"You're joking," Buckskin said. "I told you I shot him in the leg and then the rattler bit him five or six times."

"Yep, what you told me. Only my deputies found a different story when they got up there this afternoon. They found Pickering with not one but two slugs through his head, one from the side, the other close by on the back of his head that left powder burns. Now just keep your hands in the air while I relieve you of that iron and then you'll have a nice soft mattress in our jail cell."

Buckskin kept his hands in the air. This couldn't be. "Which deputy found the body? Bring that lying son-of-a-bitch in here. I want to talk to him."

The barrel of a six-gun slammed into Buckskin's right kidney and he went down on his knees, gagging, trying to keep from throwing up.

"I found him, big timer," the deputy behind Buckskin said. He was the man who had just swung his revolver. "I'm deputy Quantrill Norton and I found him with two slugs in his head. You admitted you were there, that you chased him and that you shot him. That makes you the killer and we'll prove it in court. Now, think you can walk into the cell block or you want me to kick your butt all the damn way?"

Buckskin stood with a lot of concentration and a determined effort. He took one look at the man behind him, a deputy he had seen in the office before. He was big and tall, wore a full beard, and had jagged black stumps for teeth.

"I can walk," Buckskin said, not quite sure how he spoke the words without vomiting. He shuffled back to the cell and slumped on the bare wood of the bunk along one stone wall. It was a half hour before he felt like talking.

He had been thinking how to clear himself. It would be hard. The deputy had put the slugs into Pickering's head. But why? On orders? Whose?

He thought about it until his head hurt, then at last he came up with a possible reason for the frame up. He rattled the bars until a deputy stuck his head around the corner.

"I need to see Doc Ralston. I'm bleeding from my gunshot wound."

The deputy frowned. "I'll talk to the sheriff."

Ten minutes later the sawbones came down the corridor with a deputy and stepped into the cell when the door opened. The lawman locked the iron bars behind him.

The doctor looked at him curiously. "Your wound break open?"

Buckskin nodded and the medic told him to pull down his pants so he could take a look. The deputy wandered back to the front and left them alone.

Buckskin whispered to the medic and they both sat on the bench.

"The sheriff is framing me for killing Pickering. I'm not sure why, but there should be a way to prove I didn't do it. Now hear me out. Do you have any influence on the sheriff?

"Some. I helped get him elected."

"Good. Here's my only defense, and you're the only man in town who can clear me. Don't let them bury Pickering's body or dispose of it in any way. I want you to examine it. You have to do that anyway as the county coroner, don't you?"

The doctor nodded.

"Tell me why a body bleeds, doctor."

"Easy, the blood in a body is under pressure. Blood pressure, we call it. We can measure it now. When a hole gets punched in one of the veins or arteries or any of the smaller tubes, the blood pressure forces blood out the hole."

"What happens with a dead body?"

"Easy again. A dead body doesn't bleed. Say you slash a guy with a knife across his gut. He'll bleed like crazy. But once he dies, the blood stops flowing. There's no pump—the heart—working to force the blood out."

"So, can you tell if a body is stabbed or shot after it's dead?"

"Oh, absolutely. It's a simple matter of checking to see if the wound has bled or not."

Buckskin nodded grimly. "That would be true of a head shot as well?"

"Yes, without question."

"Okay, Dr. Ralston. They say I shot Pickering in the head twice, killing him. Actually he died of six rattler bites but mostly from shock and fright. I'd guess his heart gave out. He had one bleeding wound on his leg. But I'm staking my life on the fact that those two head shots will show that they came some time, three or four hours, after Pickering was already dead."

The doctor nodded. "Yep, if Jefferson set this up, he's got some big deal going somewhere. The man works everyone for everything he can."

139

"What about the railroad men in town? First Baines had the job of helping them. He got murdered. Pickering admitted he killed him to get the rights to help the rail men. Then Pickering is dead and I'm the one who watched him die, but I'm also a fly in the cider for what the Sheriff now wants to do, take over the Pickering job with the railroad men."

"Figures. That damn railroad has already caused this town more trouble than it's gonna be worth. I'll get out of here and take a look at the body, then go straight to Circuit Court Judge Oswald who came into town this afternoon. He's an honest man. Might take a few hours, but you should be out before nightfall."

Doc Ralston put away things in his black bag and rattled the bars to attract the attention of the deputy. He came briskly, let the doctor out and scowled at Buckskin who had stretched out on the hard wood of the bunk.

A half hour later, the bearded deputy sheriff came with the keys and rousted Buckskin.

"First hearing before Judge Oswald," the lawman said. "He's gonna set your trial date for tomorrow to give a lawyer lots of time to prepare your defense. Come on, you killer. Been more than two years since we had a honest to God hanging in this town. Looks like we got one for sure now."

Buckskin figured the medic would be there, but he wasn't. The judge sat at a desk in the sheriff's office and stared at a piece of paper. He looked up at Buckskin who had been placed in handcuffs and stood before the judge.

"Young man, are you Lee Morgan?"

"Yes sir."

"You are charged with murder in the case of the death of Adler Pickering, a member of the court residing in Jackson. You are charged with shooting him twice in the head and claiming that he died of a rattlesnake bite. What do you have to say in your defense?"

Buckskin outlined the bushwhacking near the stable, how he took the horse and gave chase and how at last the lawyer had died from fear, fright or shock when the hated rattlesnake bit him five or six times.

"So you swear you didn't kill the man?"

"Absolutely your honor, and I can prove it. I'm not quite ready to show you that proof yet, but soon."

"You have a revolver?"

"They took it away from me when they arrested me."

"I hear there's a new way to look through a microscope and see the little lines on a lead bullet when it leaves the barrel of a gun. By test firing the same gun into some soft material, such as packed cotton, you can get a bullet you know came from a given gun and compare the little scratch marks on it with those on the bullet from the victim. Would you like to have such a test made on your gun?"

"Yes, sir, your honor. Also, such a test should be made on the weapon carried by Deputy Quantrill Norton, who is the one who shot the victim in the head."

"Very well. The problem is, young man, that we don't have that kind of equipment. It's still experimental and I don't know if I would allow such evidence to be submitted even if we had it. There's no precedent for such evidence. So, from the sworn evidence by law officers and the given facts I have before me, I'll bind you over to trial. Trial date set a week from today."

Buckskin saw the sheriff standing to one side.

Dr. Ralston stood up near the back of the room. "Your honor, if I could have a moment with the prisoner. His leg wound seems to need some attention. He was shot, as you know, by the dead man. It will only take a minute or two."

"Well, Newton, that seems reasonable. You take your time. We don't have that dinner set until six-thirty, I think we said. I'll see you there."

Dr. Ralston walked beside Buckskin as they went back to the cell. Once safely locked inside and the deputy gone back down the corridor, the medic grinned.

"I had a long look at the deceased. There is absolutely no doubt that the bullet holes in Pickering's head were made at least four hours after he died. I can tell that because of the no bleeding after death proof, and from the condition of the body. I shouldn't have any trouble convincing Judge Oswald that you could not have killed the man. I used to practice down in Rock Springs when Judge Oswald was a lawyer down there."

"I hope you can do it, Doc. You're the only defense I've got. Even the circumstantial evidence they have would probably be enough to convince a jury."

"It'll never come to a trial." The sawbones stood. "Now I better get out of here and clear out my waiting room patients so I won't be late for dinner with the judge."

142

Buckskin ate the meal they brought him, a bowl of stew, two slabs of bread and coffee. It was better than he had expected.

About seven-thirty by his pocket watch, he heard some loud voices in the outer rooms of the sheriff's office. A minute or two later, a deputy rushed into the aisle between the cells, ran down to Buckskin and unlocked his cell.

"Come on," the deputy said, but he didn't touch Buckskin or push him. His face looked pale.

In the sheriff's private office the lawman and Deputy Quantrill Norton stood ramrod stiff in front of Judge Oswald who now sat in the sheriff's chair. He looked over at Buckskin as he came into the room.

"Oh, Morgan. You're free to go. All charges against you have been dropped and will be deleted from any permanent records." He looked back at the sheriff.

"Jefferson, you are hereby relieved of your office and your official duties until a grand jury investigation is completed. You and Deputy Quantrill Norton are both under the severest reprimand. Criminal charges will be filed against you as soon as I can talk to the district attorney. You both are released from custody under your own warrant. I advise both of you to stay within the county. If I catch you so much as a foot outside the county line I'll run you down to Rock Springs and throw you in the worst cells I can find. Are we clear on this?"

The two men nodded.

"Your honor, I'd like my weapon back. Then I have a thing or two to discuss with you about the death of Elwood Baines."

# Kit Dalton

The judge nodded. "Tomorrow will be time enough. I've got a wild game of pinochle planned for tonight. Tomorrow, my hotel room, ten o'clock sharp."

Buckskin nodded. He headed for Josh Baines' cafe to catch him up on the news.

# Chapter Eleven

The night passed quickly for Buckskin. He got to bed early, went right to sleep and didn't wake up until 6:30 the next morning. He had no idea where Tilly was, and he was glad he had a chance for some good solid sleep.

When he tried to get out of bed the next morning, his left leg was so stiff he yoweled in pain. He struggled for what seemed like five minutes to get the leg working properly. He was still limping slightly when he stiff-legged walked down the stairs a half hour later.

A visit to Doc Ralston proved helpful. The sawbones put fresh salve on the wounds and rebandaged them. Then he put a hot brick in a cloth sack and placed it on Buckskin's leg above and below the wound. Almost at once the stiffness and soreness vanished.

"How did you do that?" Buckskin asked.

The doctor showed him the bricks and grinned. "Old Indian trick I learned one summer when I was friends with some reservation redskins. I learned a lot during those two months."

Buckskin arrived at the Judge's room at the hotel fifteen minutes early but was invited inside.

"Nice piece of work on the sheriff yesterday," Judge Oswald said. "On paper he had you all ready to hang. How in hell did you come up with that bleed, no bleed idea?"

"I've seen enough bodies in my time, your honor, to know what goes on with the dead ones. But without Doc Ralston's expert medical testimony, I might have been hung."

"Ralston is a good man. Now, you wanted to talk about Baines. I sat in on a session with the sheriff two weeks ago when we went over the Baines murder. He said he had no evidence of any kind one way or the other that would lead to any suspects who could be convicted."

"Adler Pickering is the man who shot Baines in the head," Buckskin said. "He admitted it to me yesterday and I wanted to bring him back to town for a trial to clear up the Baines death, but he panicked and tried to run away and stepped on the rattler. I'll file a deposition as to what the dead man said to me if that will help clear up the matter."

"Help, yes, but it might not finish it."

"Two other things, Judge. Doc Ralston said that Baines had been poisoned as well as shot. His lips had turned blue by the next morning, and the Doc said it was strychnine. He figured if the six-gun had not been used, that Baines would have died from the poison within a half hour after he was shot."

"So, the question is, young man, who really killed Baines, the gunshot or the poison. I can rule on that right now. If the victim was still alive at the time of the gunshot, that bullet is what killed him. The poison might have done the job in another half hour, but the poisoner could be charged only with attempted murder."

Judge Oswald stared at Buckskin. "You seem to know a lot about this case. Do you know who poisoned Baines?"

"No sir, but I have a suspicion. If it turns out to be true, then what am I to do?"

"I'll let you be the judge of that, Morgan. If you believe that the person should be prosecuted for attempted murder, then file the needed complaint with the district attorney. On the other hand, if you think that justice has taken its course over this one death, then perhaps you can look the other way and let it pass. You're not a member of the court, so you're not required to follow through. If I knew about it, I would be required to take action."

"The same idea hold for the shotgunning of Baines?"

"I'd say so. Those wounds could have caused death if he had not reached a doctor. He was killed with the derringer slug you said before that time. Therefore, the shotgunning could classify as assault with a deadly weapon or attempted murder, either one of which could bring ten year sentences in the territorial prison."

147

# Kit Dalton

The judge paused and looked out the window. "Justice in these frontier towns is tough enough, but when the suspects pile up and the reasons for killing one man multiply, it's time to settle down and reduce the case to the least common criminal, deal with him and pass on the rest. When I get your deposition on Pickering's confession, I'll declare the case of the Baines murder closed."

Buckskin thanked the judge, went downstairs and walked up Main toward the town house owned now by Mrs. Baines, or more properly, Widow Baines. He saw movement at one of the ground floor room curtains but couldn't identify the person. He strolled up the walkway to the front door and twisted the device on the outside of the wall that rang a bell inside.

The door opened slowly, then came inward all the way.

"Why, Mr. Morgan, you've come back to see me. I expect that you want to collect your five-thousand dollars now that you've discovered who killed my husband."

"That would please me, Mrs. Baines. I've talked with Judge Oswald and he assures me that the confession of Adler Pickering closes the case of the death of Elwood Baines."

She beamed. He noticed that she wore a party dress that was cut low so the sides of both her breasts showed. She had her hair piled on top of her head and had a few touches of pinkness applied to her cheeks and her lips.

"Please come this way and I'll give you a draft on the bank. There is plenty of money to cover it and I've told the banker that you'll be in today."

# Derringer Danger

They went to what must have been the beginnings of a study that Baines had been developing. It had oak bookcases on one side and the head of an eight-point deer on the other wall. Mrs. Baines sat down at the desk, took an envelope from under the blotter and handed it to Buckskin.

"Now I want you to look at it, to inspect the draft to be sure that it's signed and all is in order."

Buckskin opened the envelope, looked at the draft and saw that it had been made payable to him and was in the amount of $5,000.

"Yes, ma'am, it looks all correct and proper. I thank you."

"It's money well spent because now I know for sure who killed my husband."

"I understand he was your husband in name only, Mrs. Baines. Had you shut him out of your bed?"

She shuddered a moment, then stood, caught his hand and led him into a sitting room. She dropped on a couch, pulling him down beside her.

"That's all so old and ugly. I don't want to talk about it."

"Why did you push him out of your marriage bed, Mrs. Baines?"

"Oh hell. If I tell you, will that satisfy your curiosity, and then we can get on with more interesting things?"

"Yes, I really need to know. Was he a bad lover?"

Raquel Baines laughed. "No, not in any way. Elwood was a dramatic and tender lover. He knew exactly what to do to make me want him to take me. That's eventually what caused the trouble. I'd had two children. I didn't want anymore. The only

149

way I knew to prevent having children was to abstain from intercourse.

"I told him this and he said there were other methods. But he didn't tell me any and I'd never heard of any that worked. So I told him no more lovemaking.

"He put up with it for a while, then he began going to town in the evening and I knew he was trying out the local whores. At first I was angry, then I realized it took the strain off him and meant I didn't have to fight him off. What had been a simple way to not have children soon turned into a way of life, and we simply lived under the same roof but slept in separate bedrooms and never were intimate."

She stood and motioned to him. "Let's go to the kitchen and have something to drink. I'm partial to coffee, but you can have tea or whatever you want."

"Coffee will be fine."

They went into the kitchen and she put a coffee pot on an already banked fire. She put the coffee grounds in and they settled down at the table to let the brew boil.

"Weren't you a little jealous knowing your husband was having his way with the women in town?"

"Not at all. Not for four or five years. Then I learned a few things about timing and when not to go to bed with a man so I wouldn't get pregnant. I wanted him back, but by that time the gulf was too deep and he simply wasn't interested in me anymore. Lord knows that I tried. He told me that I could live here and help raise our children, but that was the end of it for him."

"So what did you do?"

"I turned into my shell. Hardly ever went out. I

didn't need to watch the women talking about me, hear the whispers. I just stayed home and took care of my children and concentrated on running the house."

She checked on the coffee. "It's going to take a few minutes more. Why don't we go back in the parlor where it's more comfortable?"

They did. They talked some more and then she stood quickly. "Oh, the coffee must be ready. You stay here, I'll be right back. Do you want a cookie to go with the coffee?"

He said he did and she hurried into the kitchen. Quickly she came back with the coffee pot on a tray, two cups and a plate of cookies. She poured them each a cup and she tasted it. Or did she? Buckskin watched her without appearing to do so. He had a corner of one of the cookies and pretended to drink some coffee.

Coffee? Was she going to poison him, too? Was the drink laced with strychnine?

"When you called before, I decided to prove to you that I'm not one of those women who doesn't like sex. You left too quickly, but I'm ready to show you again, right now."

She moved beside him on the couch and lifted her skirts until they were gathered around her waist, showing her high stockings and a stretch of pink leg between their tops and her soft blue bloomers.

"I have good legs, don't you think?"

"Mrs. Baines, this isn't necessary. You don't have to prove anything to me."

"Oh, but I do. I must make you understand that I'm not cold and sexless, that I have feelings." She pulled the bodice of her dress apart and spread it back so he could see one breast with its softly pink areola and nipple. "Does my body excite you, Lee Morgan?"

"You know it does."

She took his hand and placed it over her breast. "Then encourage me, at least say you like my breasts."

Her hands reached for his crotch, found the growing erection behind his fly and rubbed it. She opened the buttons on his fly and snaked out his penis that was half erect.

"My, what a beautiful one. I want him inside me. Right now, Morgan. Right here on the couch."

She bent and slid down her bloomers, then lay on her back on the couch with one leg on the floor, the other one over the back rest.

"Right now, Morgan. Right this second!"

By then he was ready. He moved over her, let her guide him inside and then drove forward as she screeched in pain and anger and joy and rapture all rolled into one. The searing of dry flesh came only once, then her juices flowed and they meshed as her hips pumped up against him.

Buckskin shook his head as he pounded into the woman harder and harder, not waiting for her, not worrying about her, only surging to his own satisfaction.

She erupted into a wild, screaming climax before he did. It caught him by surprise and urged him on. A moment later he exploded and drove her higher on the couch with each dramatic thrust. The final one came and he blasted her deep into the couch with his final thrust, then he relaxed and let himself down on top of her.

Her arms locked around his shoulders, pinning them together.

"Oh, God, yes! How much I've been missing. Hell, I can have almost any unattached man I want in town now. Who will want to say no to me? I can tease them and seduce them, or I can hire them as male studs to service me. Damn but this is going to be fine."

Twenty minutes later, they had pulled their clothes back in order and sat on the couch. She pretended to sip at her coffee but he could see the level was the same. He pointed at one of the windows.

"Did I see someone out there looking in?"

"Oh, gracious, I hope not. I'll go take a peek."

As soon as she walked away, he poured his coffee down the crack between the couch cushion and the end. The he sloshed out more until the cup was nearly empty.

When she came back saying she saw no one, he took the cup down from his mouth and showed it to her.

"Another cup?" he asked. "All that poking made me thirsty."

She frowned for a minute, then lifted her brows. "No, I think one cup is enough for you. I want to be sure you know that I'm not frigid like an icicle. I want you to know that I found out who he was fucking in town. I knew about Irene, about Patsy, about three or four others. All young girls. Young and new, and he probably taught them how to fuck just exactly the way he wanted them to.

"I stood it as long as I could. Then when he said he was going into town that final night, I decided that was the time. I made him supper and coffee as usual, only I put an added spice into his coffee."

"You poisoned him?" Buckskin said slurring his words.

She smiled. "That I did. Good, fast-acting rat poison. Works in about forty-five minutes. He had two cups that night and I told him I wanted tea instead. Midge never drinks coffee so there was no danger. He had his two cups and I waved goodbye to him knowing I'd never see him alive again.

"Oh, you don't need to worry about telling anyone what I'm saying. You drank enough coffee to take care of two men your size.

"Yes, I wanted Elwood dead and I poisoned him to make it happen. Then somebody shot him. Two people shot him, but the damn lawyer he trusted put his derringer to his head and blew him into hell before my poison would work. That's why I wanted you to find out for me who shot Elwood."

"What now?" Buckskin said, the words so faint and slurred he could hardly hear them himself.

"What now? You'll die, of course. I'll wait until dark and take the buggy and drop you off in a canyon somewhere. Be weeks before anyone finds you. Too bad, you were a good fuck. I enjoyed that. I used a few of the cowboys, but they don't have your drive, your flat out raw sex appeal. Good-bye, darling. I hate to watch a man die."

Buckskin stood and grinned. "Don't worry about me dying, Mrs. Baines. I'm a long way from it. And don't reach for the derringer you probably hid under the cushions. I wouldn't want you to get your hand all wet where I poured out your coffee. That poison was so strong I could smell it when you brought in the cups. I should insist you have a few pulls on your coffee just to see how you like the taste."

"No!" she said so quickly that Buckskin grinned.

"You'll have your day in court. Judge Oswald left it up to me. I'm going to write out a complaint against you for attempted murder of your husband. I'll let the district attorney decide what he's going to do with it. You might go to prison for ten years. Your son and daughter will run the ranch. Probably do a better job of it than you ever could."

He went to the front door and unlatched it. "You probably will want to stay in town until the district attorney talks to you. He might see it differently, who knows? Oh, and don't try to stop payment on that draft. I'm going right down to the bank now and get my money. I earned it."

He turned and walked out the front door, down the steps to the street and walked quickly to the bank where he took ten five-hundred dollar bills from the banker in exchange for the draft. Back in his hotel room, he dug out the money belt from his portmanteau and fitted the ten $500-bills inside, strapping it around his stomach to make sure it didn't show. Then he headed to see the district attorney in the courthouse.

The lawman shook his head when Buckskin told him the story. "The undertaker, Horatio Weaver, will confirm the color of the dead man's lips, and Dr. Ralston will also testify about strychnine poisoning. He saw the body as well and noted the color when he did the coroner's report."

"So what the hell am I supposed to do, haul the town's richest woman into court for attempted murder?"

"She did try to kill the man. I'll stay around for the trial if you want me to. You have my testimony and the medical opinion of Dr. Ralston. What more do you need?"

The district attorney was a middle sized man, soft and pale in appearance, with longish brown hair that fell down over his eyes. He kept swiping at it with one hand and trying to write on a pad with his other hand.

His name was Henshaw and he was in his second four-year term. People Buckskin had talked to said he was honest and conscientious.

"You have any idea how hard it would be to find an impartial jury of twelve men from this town? Half of them work for her or the stores she owns. Even if I could find twelve, they could just as soon say the body's lips turned blue because he got too cold and say that you're an outsider who came to town to find a killer and that you killed the man yourself. I'd give odds of twenty-to-one right now that I couldn't get a guilty verdict on charges against Mrs. Baines."

Buckskin stood and watched the man. "So what are you going to do? You know now that she would have been a killer if Pickering hadn't selected that same night to take out his wrath on his client. Twenty minutes more, maybe less, and Raquel Baines would have succeeded in killing her husband.

"I know you have the good of the community to think about. Fine. I'd suggest that you talk to Judge Oswald today before or after your court session and get his advice on this matter. He seemed to me to be an honest man and one with a well developed sense of justice.

"You let me know. I did what I figured I had to do. Now it's up to you. If you want me to stay for a trial, I'll stay for a week, even two. The decision is up to you."

Buckskin turned and walked out of the courthouse. He found Josh Baines getting ready for the noon rush at his Grand Teton Cafe. Buckskin had a cup of coffee and tasted it critically, passed it and took a swallow.

Over the next hour he told Baines everything he had found out about the case, including the story about Irene and about Raquel Baines and her poison laced coffee.

Josh nodded. "Figured about Raquel. I never did understand that woman. I don't think Elwood did either. She always was a little strange. The surprise is Elwood and the young girls. Damn, I'd never have thought it of him."

He served some sandwiches on plates and two orders of beef stew and pushed them out on the counter for his one waitress to deliver.

"How much did you say Elwood stood to gain by pushing the railroad into town?"

"Near as I can recall, fifty-thousand cash and the deeds to two-hundred, mile-square sections of Wyoming land along the rails."

"Well, that's a pile of money. At least it's enough to get killed over. That poor bastard. If he hadn't pushed so hard, hadn't made so many damn deadly enemies, he'd still be alive today."

Josh wiped his hands on his stained apron. "Okay, you found the killer like I asked you to. How much do I owe you?"

Buckskin scratched his head and squinted up his

eyes. "You gave me some expense money as I recall. You picked me up when I was lower on the pole than a two ounce flea hound. Then too, I've been eating free in here for several days. I'd say we're just about even."

Josh looked at him and his face twisted into a lopsided grin. "Be damned, you must have squeezed some cash out of that wild woman, my favorite sister-in-law."

Buckskin took a long pull at his coffee, then nodded. "Indeed, my good man, I did. She came asking me, weren't none of my push. But then I didn't turn down her greenbacks either once I had the killer pegged."

Josh grinned again and cleaned the grill of grease with his spatula. "Damn, I won't insult you by asking you how much she paid you, but I'd bet a double eagle it was more than you were charging me."

Buckskin laughed and nodded. "Considerably, but I figured that she could afford it."

"So, you're clear of us here at Jackson in the back sticks of Wyoming."

"Not quite. Need to do some talking in a deposition and have somebody write it down. Then too, the D.A. might want me to hang around for a trial. Don't know for sure. I figure he'll have it worked out by tomorrow."

"What are you going to do, gamble away your hard earned pay?"

"Not by a damn sight. I want to know who in town is the best fisherman, and talk him into taking me over to the Snake so I can try for some of those cutthroat trout that are supposed to be the best in the world. I hear that fly fishing is the way to catch those cutthroats, that right?"

"Best fisherman in town?"

"Right, somebody who can show me where to fish, maybe have a boat and some fly rods, and know which flies are best for this time of year."

"Best fisherman with a boat and equipment and who knows all the best spots to fish. That's probably me."

Buckskin grinned and held out his hand. "How about tomorrow bright and early. You get somebody to do the cooking for you here in your place and we'll go bring in a string of trout."

# Chapter Twelve

Only one change had to be made in the plans for the fishing trip the next morning. Tilly got the day off from working at the hotel and insisted on going along. She said she had been fishing dozens of times and could swing a fly rod better than most men could.

She wore jeans and a plaid shirt, half boots and a grin as wide as the Wyoming sky.

Josh looked at her and shrugged. They would float down the Snake, anchor near shore in spots and fish up a storm. Josh had hitched two horses to a light wagon that carried the three of them and a ten-foot rowboat on it. He had a spotted mare tied on the back that didn't care much for the trip but put up with it. A driver went along and would drop them off at the river three miles due west of town, then go downstream on the river trail to the south road

and meet them at a place some were starting to call
Hoback Junction. It was near where the Teton River
dumped into the growing Snake.

Josh had brought four fly fishing poles, long slender
sticks made flexible enough to whip a light fly line
back and forth several times before the fisherman
dropped the fly exactly in the riffle or the surge of
current where he wanted it.

"You fished before?" Josh asked Tilly.

She grinned and touched Josh's shoulder. "Yes
indeed, Josh Baines. I've been fishing all my life,
I reckon. Fly fishing is just one of the kinds of
fishing I do."

She shrugged and they pushed off from a calm spot
along the shore in the boat. Josh manned the oars and
dropped his pair of iron window sash weights for an
anchor ten feet off shore in a little backwater, shipped
his oars and picked up one of the fly poles.

"Easy using one of these things," he said. He
whipped a yellow and white fly back and forth,
letting out more and more line from the reel until
at last he had thirty feet of line zinging back and forth
until he dropped the fly in the edge of the current and
let it ride downstream.

"Fish are working upstream this time of year, so
you let the food come to them," Josh said. He grinned.
The tip of his pole jerked downward and he lifted the
pole sharply, then laughed and began working the fish
toward the boat.

It was a short, splashing fight, but Josh maneuvered
the trout close and then lifted it into the boat.

"Cutthroat, about eleven inches long," Josh said. "A
keeper. Now, I want both of you to practice with those

161

poles so you can do some good when we hit the fast water."

They both worked at flipping the fly back and forth. Tilly had been true to her word. She worked the fly line as well as Josh had and dropped her fly into the edge of the current but didn't get a bite. She pulled the line in and tried again.

Buckskin had more trouble with the whip motion and settled for a 20-foot cast. To his surprise the fly vanished in a large splash as soon as it hit the water and line whined off his reel.

"Got a good one," Josh called.

Buckskin had fished before. Now with a fish on line, he knew what to do. He pumped the fish toward the boat, lifting the pole upward and then lowering it while he reeled in as fast as he could.

"That's a lunker," Josh shouted. "Must go at least three pounds. Don't loose him."

Buckskin pumped the rod upward again, felt the strain on the thin leader that held the hook, and then suddenly there was no pressure at all.

"Lost him," Josh said. "Don't be in so much of a hurry. We've got all day to catch a bucket full."

They moved down the river and all three made small fish catches. Then Josh rowed for the shore. He grounded the boat and stepped into a foot of water.

"So, you two, go have a good day of fishing. I've got to get back to work. Only got a man to cook for four hours. By the time I find the horse that Charlie left for me and get back to town, I'll be due to go back to work."

"Thought you were going to show us the best holes to fish," Buckskin said.

"Don't look like you need no instruction that way. Charlie will pick you up whenever you show up down at the junction. I'll see you whenever you get back to the cafe." He waved, turned and walked away upstream toward where they had put the boat in the water.

Buckskin had been on the oars. He pushed off and angled into the water, then anchored near shore and they both cast into the current. Almost at the same time they both hooked trout and they laughed and yelled as they worked the hard fighting cutthroat trout near enough to the boat to lift them over the side.

"My pa always used a net to catch the fish once he got it near enough to the boat or shore," Tilly said.

Buckskin tried another cast and came up empty so he pulled in the anchor and they drifted down another fifty yards to another promising spot. The boat was twenty yards off shore when the anchor went down. The water here was deceptively deep, maybe ten feet, Buckskin estimated.

He had taken his gunbelt off and folded it in the bow wrapped in his jacket. It was summer warm by that time of morning. Tilly hooked a fish but lost it almost at once and she cast again.

Buckskin was about to cast when the boat wobbled in the current and he heard a rifle shot from the near shore. A bullet whispered a foot from his chest and he bellowed at Tilly to get down.

"Flat in the bottom of the boat!" he roared. Buckskin had bellied down and stretched for his weapon in the bow. He pulled it out when another rifle shot jolted through the side of the boat but missed him. He peered over the top of the rowboat's side, saw the white blush of smoke from some brush on shore and fired twice into the haze.

It was too far to be accurate with a six-gun but it might slow them down a little. He pulled his knife and cut the bow anchor rope, dropping the anchor into the river and letting the craft lurch downstream. Another shot came from the same spot on shore but it missed.

"Who in hell is shooting at us?" Tilly rasped.

"Wish I knew. We've got to get to shore without becoming sitting duck targets. Keep low."

He lifted one of the oars and used it over the stern as a rudder to steer the boat toward shore. He heard the sound of revolver rounds, but two or three of them failed to reach the boat.

Another minute and they were close enough to shore to see the bottom. Still too deep to walk. He hunkered down but had to have a shoulder and arm over the side of the boat to use the oar as a rudder.

A rifle shot sounded and at almost the same instant he felt his shoulder smash forward. He dropped the oar and fell into the bottom of the boat. His left shoulder gouted with blood. Tilly screamed and crawled to him. She pushed her handkerchief over the bloody path of the bullet.

Buckskin shook his head and looked at his wound. Not all that bad. The heavy caliber slug had gouged a ditch through the top of his shoulder, missing the bone, but tearing through a dozen muscles. The arm would be of little use to him for several days.

He felt the boat hit bottom and he looked at Tilly. He stuffed three more rounds into his weapon to give him six loads. Then he checked the girl again. "When

I say go, you slip over the side of the boat downstream into the water and run like hell for the trees. I'll be slamming six rounds into the trees and brush upstream to keep them from shooting at you. Are you ready?"

Tilly nodded. Her upper teeth clamped on her lower lip and he saw the anger and determination in her eyes.

"Slip over the side, now!"

She went over and a rifle sounded but the round missed her.

"Move to the front of the boat but stay low and out of sight. When I fire the first round, you run like crazy for the brush."

Buckskin turned and lifted his six-gun's barrel over the side of the wooden boat. He saw movement twenty yards upstream and he fired. He felt her move but didn't have time to watch. He fired again, then again, waited a few seconds and saw new brush movement. He fired the fourth round, then the fifth. He paused and saw a man dash from the brush toward a tree. He tracked him, gave him a little lead and fired. The heavy slug caught the runner in the chest and stopped him like a freight train hitting the end of the tracks.

Somewhere near by he thought he heard a cry, but he wasn't sure. He reloaded with one hand, then eased over the back side of the boat as Tilly had done and dropped into the ice cold water. He paused, then surged ahead running forward, looking upstream. Twice he fired where brush moved, then he was into the growth of a few small cottonwood and a lot of aspen. He called softly for Tilly and she answered from behind a two-foot thick cottonwood.

Buckskin rushed that way. He saw her pale face first, then the bloodstain high on the left side of her chest.

"Got hit," she said and almost passed out.

He reloaded and knelt beside her, both safe for the moment. She was hit bad. He didn't know if it would be fatal, but he had to stop the bleeding. Might be bleeding inside, too.

He touched the wound on her chest, then eased her away from the tree and looked at her back. A splotch of bloody shirt six inches wide showed where the bullet had come out.

"Oh, damn!" She was in critical condition. Doc Ralston might be able to save her if he were here. He lifted his six-gun and looked around the tree at ground level. He saw a bearded man holding a rifle at port arms, walking forward. He had a red kerchief around his throat and had on green pants and shirt. He stepped into the open, stalking them. Why?

Another ten feet, Buckskin silently thought. Another six. Come on. The man stopped and surveyed the ground ahead of him. He dropped to one knee, scanned the area, evidently looking for any sign of movement or color. Then, evidently satisfied, he rose and walked ahead, rifle now aiming forward, his finger on the trigger.

Buckskin Morgan fired twice so fast that the second bullet hit the man's chest before the first one had killed him. He flopped backward from the force of the two heavy rounds and died without making a sound.

Buckskin eased back behind the tree. Tilly stared at him and he wasn't sure if she was alive or dead.

"Get him?" she whispered.

"Got him. Two of them down." He looked around the tree again. Nothing else upstream moved. He looked to the side, away from the stream. Someone might have gone around to get them in a crossfire. He listened. The only thing he could hear was the labored wheezing breath coming from Tilly. He tried to shut it out.

She moaned and her head lowered gently toward her chest. She lifted one hand and covered the small, deadly wound.

He watched to the side, then downstream. They were at risk that way. But was there another ambusher upstream as well? He took another look upstream.

The fraction of a second that his head eased around the cottonwood, a shotgun blasted one barrel at him. He tried to pull back, but the bird shot pellets thundered into the tree and two grazed off the top of his head. One embedded in his forehead but it didn't hurt. It must have hit something else first.

Somewhere along the way he had lost his hat. He checked his loads in his Colt: still six, and maybe fifteen rounds left in the loops on his gun belt.

Two rifles and a shotgun. Who wanted him dead that badly? He could think of only one, and a woman at that: Raquel Baines. She had to be behind it. She'd simply hire three or four gunmen and give them a target. They wouldn't care if they killed a young girl in the process.

How many of them? Three? Four? He heard a sound downstream and shot his glance that way. Nothing moved. The chatter of the Snake was lower here, a stretch with little white water and few rocks extending above the surface.

Buckskin listened again. Yes, another noise downstream. Someone approached his position from that direction. He sectioned the green growth and tall cottonwoods off and examined one part of it at a time. The second time he examined the whole area he saw brush move thirty yards away, slightly toward the stream. An old cottonwood deadfall lay in that direction only a few feet from him. He eased Tilly down to a prone position and pushed her over two feet so she was behind the rotting cottonwood log that was nearly three feet thick.

Upstream.

He looked around the tall cottonwood on the left side this time. Nothing moved. The smoke from the shotgun round had long since vanished upward in the green leaves. Someone was out there. Another killer crept toward him from the other direction.

Survival, the first law.

He checked the spot downstream where he had noticed movement. Still out of his range, but an easy shot for a rifleman. Should he go to the big log for protection from downstream, or be more concerned with the shotgun upstream?

The decision came for him when a man downstream stood and fired three times with the rifle as fast as he could. One round hit the tree above Buckskin. The second clipped his pants leg but didn't cut flesh, and the third went into the air because Buckskin had lofted his six-gun barrel and fired four times at the shooter.

One of the rounds hit him in the left eye and drilled him backwards into the greenery. Buckskin nodded, reloaded and looked upstream again.

A long, low wail came from the brush. Then the wail changed to a scream and a wild figure dressed in clothes too large and holding a shotgun charged out of the brush and straight at the tree where Buckskin crouched. The shotgun fired once, but Buckskin was out of sight. He looked around and fired his own weapon. The .45 slug hit the runner in the left thigh and he went down, rolled and fired the second barrel of the shotgun.

Buckskin had time to pull back behind the tree. When he looked out the next time the gunner worked frantically to reload the scatter weapon.

He had the high cards.

"Hold it right there. Drop the shotgun and live a few days longer."

The person with the weapon ignored him. Buckskin sighted in and fired. The round hit the shotgunner's upper chest as the long gun came up. A trigger finger pulled and the pellets thundered into the ground two-feet in front of the shooter.

Buckskin came out of his hiding spot and charged. He kicked the shotgun away and ripped the big hat off the man's head.

It wasn't a man.

"Hello, Raquel. I didn't know you were so good with a Greener. Afraid you won't be able to use one again for a long time." He jerked her to her feet and with her right arm twisted behind her back, he marched her down to the big cottonwood tree that had saved his life.

Buckskin pushed her to the ground and knelt beside Tilly. She blinked open her eyes and stared at him a minute.

"Beautiful dream," she said. Her words came slow and slurred. "Beautiful dream, Buckskin. Thanks for the dream."

She cried out then in terrible pain and lifted halfway to a sitting position before she shivered and cried out again. Her hand reached out and caught his in a tight grip. Then she sighed and he heard the death rattle come from her lungs as the last bit of breath gushed out of her.

Buckskin turned and backhanded Raquel Baines, slamming her to the ground, bringing a cry of pain from the woman.

"So far you've killed four people today. Any reason why I shouldn't simply shoot you in the head and throw your worthless body into the Snake and let it deal with you?"

She glared at him and he could see in her eyes that she knew he would never do that. She laughed softly. "You can't prove a thing."

He heard a moan in the brush upstream.

"I think we can prove all we need to. I just found an eyewitness who will spill everything he knows not to hang like you're going to."

"You don't even know how long he'll live." She had sat up and held one hand over her swelling right cheek.

"You say one more word and I'll hit you so hard you'll wind up floating down the Snake. Now get up. Let's go look at my witness to your hiring three killers to get even with me."

The next day in Jackson, Buckskin finished his deposition for Judge Oswald on the three different cases. The judge looked at the secretary who had written down Buckskin's statements.

"Do you have it all down on paper?" the judge asked. The woman said she did and left.

"Now, Morgan. I want to urge you to stay for the Baines trial. It should be something of a landmark. I'm going to do my best to see that that woman hangs. She's a threat to the community, to the general welfare."

"How long before the trial starts?"

"I've given a Rock Springs lawyer three days to prepare his defense. Should be lots of time. By the time the district attorney gets through with the Widow Baines, there won't be a man or woman in the county who won't plead to have her hung."

"I've never seen a woman hung before, Judge."

"Neither have I, but it's long overdue for Mrs. Baines. She not only tried to kill her husband, she hired three men to kill you and wound up getting two of them shot dead, caused the death of Tilly Vanderson, and left a third man half dead but alive enough to turn state's evidence against her. She's a menace to society."

Buckskin grinned. "Here all the time I figured that a judge was supposed to be impartial, concerned with upholding the letter of the law, not prejudiced for or against either side."

"I heard that somewhere, too. But damned if I can stand by and see this woman get only a jail term. Women have the right to vote in this territory, same as men. Now they have to learn how to be responsible citizens, the same as men. They also have the right to go to prison or hang, the same as men. I want this hanging to be a message to every woman in Wyoming that if a woman stoops to murder, she'll have to pay the penalty for murder, hanging."

"Don't see how it can fail to be a message that will be understood, your honor. Now I'm late for a noon meal. I hear that I'm having some special fresh caught cutthroat trout."

An hour later, Buckskin eased back from the table at the Grand Teton Cafe and patted his stomach.

"Couldn't have done better, Josh, if I'd cooked those trout myself. I never did ask if you found your boat and fly rods?"

"Charlie rescued them for me as they floated down the river. Actually, the boat got beached a quarter-of-a-mile from the junction and Charlie walked up that way and found it. I won't have to take the price of the gear and the boat out of your pay."

"Good. Since my pay was so low, that would mean I'd wind up owing you a couple of dollars."

Josh sat down across from Buckskin.

"Sorry about Tilly. If I'd had any idea what was going to happen, I'd have stayed with you. They might not have shot at us if there were three."

"No, they would have. Raquel Baines is a vicious animal who would have done anything to kill me. Well, that phase of this experience is over. After the trial next week I can move on."

"Where to?"

"I've got a couple of spare dollars now. I might head over into Idaho and see how the old home place is doing. Maybe that sheriff who gave my pa such a bad time has retired or been shot or something. Wonder if the Spade Bit ranch is even still there by now."

"Why not go back and see?"

"I might just do that. There must be a trail across here somewhere into Idaho. You know of any of the trails that would take me to Boise?"

"Down at the general store they have a map they sell that's supposed to show Idaho, Washington and Oregon. Not sure how good it is."

Buckskin grinned. "Yeah, that sounds about right. Get that map and take me a little ride over toward the old home place."

He couldn't remember what parts of it looked like. It had been far, far too long. How could he forget something as important as the ranch where he was raised?

Yes, it was time to go home again. He had no idea what was left there, or what he could do with what he might find. But the idea of taking a look at his beginnings began to gnaw at his mind. Yes, high time he went home. Just as soon as he was through with this trial, he'd be on a good solid mount and taking the trails west and into Idaho.

Watch out, Boise. Buckskin was coming home.